# HIGH CAGE

**Center Point
Large Print**

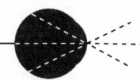

**This Large Print Book carries the
Seal of Approval of N.A.V.H.**

# HIGH CAGE

## Steve Frazee

CENTER POINT PUBLISHING
THORNDIKE, MAINE

This Center Point Large Print edition
is published in the year 2011 by arrangement with
Golden West Literary Agency.

The text of this Large Print edition is unabridged.
In other aspects, this book may vary
from the original edition.
Printed in the United States of America
on permanent paper.
Set in 16-point Times New Roman type.

ISBN: 978-1-61173-170-5

Library of Congress Cataloging-in-Publication Data

Frazee, Steve, 1909–1992.
  High cage / Steve Frazee. — Center Point large print ed.
    p. cm.
  ISBN 978-1-61173-170-5 (library binding : alk. paper)
  1. Large type books. I. Title.
  PS3556.R358H54 2011
  813′.54—dc22
                                                    2011015901

# HIGH CAGE

# Chapter 1

WE WERE on our way to the Creole Queen Mine on Bulmer Peak when the snowstorm caught us about a thousand feet above timberline. Five minutes after the first hard flakes came slicing down the wind, we could not see fifteen feet in any direction.

I had stopped to rest with Charley Spence. He was past forty-five, an old man for these parts, and he was having a bad time. His face was gray and his lips were blue and lifeless-looking. Snow had made two white patches of his brows. He was gasping as he turned his face away from the blast of the wind.

My brother Danny and Luke Fulgham were somewhere on ahead. They had left us above timberline. When I yelled for them to wait, they had pretended not to hear. By now they were probably sitting snugly in the cabin at the mine with Frank Davidson, who had gone up in good weather two days earlier.

Old Charley said, "You know where we are, Craig?"

I nodded. I knew too well where we were. Not far ahead was the High Place, where last summer I had blasted the trail across the vertical face of the mountain above Warner Basin. The very thought of the High Place was enough to tighten my stomach.

I leaned close to Charley and shouted, "We could go back to Colorow and come up later on snowshoes."

His mild brown eyes were steady under the white patches that were closing now to a solid bar across his forehead. "Yes," he said, but he was not agreeing with what I had said. "I think we can get over the High Place all right."

He meant you. Charley understood the fears of all kinds of men. That was one of the main reasons I needed him so badly at the Creole Queen. Once we reached the mine, we would be there until late spring: five men cooped up together.

I turned into the wind and started on up the icy trail.

Joe Delaverne, who was promoting the Queen, had been well pleased with my choosing Charley as one of the crew. Delaverne didn't know country rock from pine cones, but he was shrewd about men. He had been to the Queen only once, and then he like to died from the altitude.

Two summers before Delaverne had bought a prospect hole, sight unseen, from Shady Groff for two hundred bucks, and then he had hired me to show him the hole. It was only a scratch on the bleak slope of Bulmer Peak, almost at fourteen thousand feet, a small dent in granite, full of dirty-looking snow.

After a brief, unenthusiastic look at the hole, Delaverne spent the rest of his short stay on

Bulmer staring out at the pitching, bucking spines of the Flying Horse Range. With a sickly expression he said, "Jesus, that's a lot of land turned up, isn't it?"

Poking around the dump of the prospect hole, I found a pea-sized piece of calaverite, one of the richest of gold ores. Delaverne took no interest in it until we were clear off the mountain. Then he perked up and began talking a streak about promoting the Creole Queen.

That first summer he went somewhere and raised money for me to hire a crew of four men to build a trail to the Queen and to do some other work. We shot out a place for buildings near Shady's old prospect hole and got a tunnel started—smack into nothing. There was no choice: that one tiny piece of calaverite was the size of it, so I aimed the tunnel into the mountain and let it go at that. At least I headed the bore toward the highest part of Bulmer so that there would be ground overhead to stope in the unlikely event we did strike ore before we ran out of the other side of the mountain.

That was the first summer. The next year Delaverne was back. He told me to get everything ready to work a crew all winter at the mine, and then he lit out to raise more money. I built a cabin and a blacksmith shop, provisioned the cabin for five men for seven months, and had Ranald Burris and his thirty-burro packtrain haul in all the mining supplies I figured we'd need for seven months of work.

When Delaverne returned that fall he glanced at the bills I showed him and almost swallowed his cigar. "My God, Rhodes, you've ruined me!"

I tried to explain the high cost of mining. Delaverne still felt ruined. "You've got to spend it to make it," I told him.

"This is a serious matter, Rhodes!" Delaverne got up and walked clear around the poker table in Mack's place. "Put those bills in a pile. Don't leave them spread all over the table. They discourage me."

I grinned. He was likable even in the middle of his tantrum.

He sat down and lit a fresh cigar. "I didn't raise as much money as I expected this summer."

"How much of it did you lose in New Orleans?"

Delaverne shrugged. He looked helpless. "The trouble with you barbarians out here is that you have no respect for a gentleman. Now, to business. I can pay all the bills. I'll do that. But for this winter you must find a crew that will take half their wages in stock."

"Up there on Bulmer?" I shook my head.

"You must have faith, Rhodes. Perhaps we can make a small compromise, eh?"

I was suspicious. He didn't look nearly so helpless as he had a moment before.

He leaned forward and gave me his persuasive

best. "Now you, with faith in the Creole Queen, certainly will take half your wages in stock. Your younger brother, for whom it is best to be removed from Colorow for a time—"

"What do you mean, Delaverne?"

"The woman, of course. Mrs. Davidson. When she was not married—" Delaverne spread his hands and shrugged.

"How do you know?"

"I have seen."

I wasn't sure myself. Danny was nineteen. He looked older, and he had grown up fast since our father was killed in a cave-in at the Shiloh Extension. Women liked him. Lenore Enderly had liked him very much. Last week she had married Frank Davidson, and a lot of people thought he was not the man for her.

"You see?" Delaverne's look was wise and without offense. "Danny should be with you, the older brother. Perhaps the woman and her husband will be gone when you come down next spring."

"Danny is going with me, yes; but he'll never agree to take stock for half his wages."

"Say nothing of it until spring."

Delaverne had me in a crack. Both Danny and I could save money by going to the Queen. My own ambition figured in the matter too. A winter of bossing underground would put me closer to going into one of the big mines as a shifter. Fred Bannerman, the Royal Tiger owner, already had an eye on me. His daughter Bonnie and I had even talked cautiously of marriage. That was something else I would have to earn. Any way you figured it, the Queen was the place to start.

"All right, you robber," I said. "Danny and me will take half our wages in stock." I shoved the stack of bills toward Delaverne. He looked pained.

"Always bills," he said. "Let's go to Delmonico's—"

"Delmonico's is closed for alterations."

"What a savage country!"

I hired Charley as the stabilizing member of the crew. Frank Davidson wanted to go up. He said his wife was going back to the valley to finish her education at the Academy. I stalled him off. As a miner he was one of the best, but I couldn't be sure of what he suspicioned about Danny and his wife. Danny wanted me to hire Luke Fulgham, a boomer with whom Danny had taken up during the summer.

I wasn't too strong on Fulgham; he'd had too many fights around the saloons to suit me. He, too, was a good enough miner, but mining was not going to be the whole story during seven months on Bulmer. Once winter set in, no one was going out: there were no snowshoes at the Queen. I didn't want any of the crew quitting in the middle of the winter.

Bannerman put on a hundred more men at the Tiger and the Shiloh expanded operations. After that I could not be so choosy about my crew. More or less in desperation, I hired both Davidson and Fulgham. The night before we were to leave for the Queen, Danny and Fulgham went on a hell-roaring drunk and wound up in jail. It took me a day and night to get them out and then another day to get them halfway fit to climb Bulmer.

In the meantime Davidson went up on schedule.

Charley and I leaned into the wind and went on toward the High Place, following after Danny and Fulgham. We passed Coney Hollow. Twisting sheets of snow were screaming over huge blocks of granite on the upper side of the trail.

"Hold up, Craig." Charley looked worse than ever. His head was deep in the turned-up collar of his sheepskin; his face was clotted with snow; and his eyes were sick with vertigo. We rested for a few moments. He said, "You might have to help me across," and I knew he was trying to give me courage.

"Sure, Charley."

We came to the beginning of the High Place. Last summer a burro dragging timbers had gone over. Burris and I had heard a distant tinkle of rock when the animal struck the talus in Warner Basin nine hundred feet below.

Blue-white ice slanted out from the wall, forcing us to walk the outside edge of the trail. I kept leaning toward the wall, keeping my right arm extended toward it. We took ten steps. Then I saw Danny and Fulgham. Charley bumped against me lightly when I stopped.

Danny and Fulgham were sitting on the edge of the trail with their legs dangling in space. They were rocking back and forth, holding their hats on with both hands as they leaned out into the updraft from the basin. Between them was a quart bottle of whisky, almost empty. They were grinning idiotically at each other.

My toes clutched the insoles of my boots.

Danny and Fulgham drank, passing the bottle back and forth. They leaned out and spat, and their spittle went shafting above their heads in the wind. I could see that they were laughing like three-year-olds, but I could hear no sound from them.

It must have been a full ten seconds that I stood there helplessly, sick with horror. Charley said, "Let's get on across," and then I knew that he hadn't seen Danny and Fulgham. He was too close behind me, with his head lowered.

I pointed with my left hand. After a few moments I heard Charley grunt and knew that he had seen. He stepped away from me then, out toward the edge of the trail for a better look. I grabbed his arm and hauled him back. Trying to hug the wall, I slipped on the slanting ice. The split second of falling was like eternity. Charley went down with me.

Although we landed two feet from the edge, safe on solid rock, I scrabbled crazily on hands and knees to get back to the wall. I clung to a crevice, pressing my shoulder against the wall.

Charley got up slowly, weaving, dipping his head in a slow circle. I expected to see him bend in slow motion toward the drop and topple over. But he steadied his head and gained strength. The sickness seemed to leave him. He said, "Go on, Craig, and kick them across."

He could have done it himself but he knew I would forever afterward be ashamed. It was my job.

As I clung to the rock, the cold breath of the ice seemed to penetrate my bones.

Charley leaned down to me. He pointed as casually as if we were on level ground in Colorow. "That's my bottle of whisky they've got. I'm sorry I asked you to let me bring it."

No whisky at the Queen was my rule. I had made an exception for Charley because he took only an occasional tablespoon in hot water for his stomach.

"I shouldn't have brought that," Charley said.

"I'll go." I relaxed my grip until the sloping ice slid me gently, still on hands and knees, to the solid part of the trail.

Danny and Fulgham were laughing at me now. I realized the truth. When they saw Charley and me coming, they began putting on their show. I wanted to get them both on the other side, in the sliderock, and beat them until they were helpless.

As I rose, they stood up, grinning at me, and began a prancing dance, kicking their feet out over the basin. I shouted at them and cursed them, but my agitation only served to increase their merriment. Fulgham began to walk backward, leaning, imitating a drunken man who can't keep his balance.

He forgot one fact: the altitude. He was twice as drunk as he thought he was. He did fall, skidding on his seat to the edge of the drop. One leg went over. He sat there looking startled for an instant, and then hooked his arm for me to go on by him. When Danny came stumbling over to help him up, Fulgham hauled Danny down beside him, where they wrestled, laughing idiotically.

When I got beside them, I kicked Danny in the ribs. He thought Fulgham had struck him. I kicked him again, and he looked at me and scowled. Fulgham sat up. With the toe of my boot I ground a pinch of his buttock flesh against the trail. He yelped in pain.

I pointed ahead and yelled. Danny caught the idea first. He staggered up, rubbing his ribs. He went along the High Place, swooped up the bottle of whisky, and disappeared into the whirling darkness.

When I could no longer see him, I was more afraid than ever. *Oh, Christ,* he'll fall! He'll fall!

Fulgham looked at me belligerently. He was a heavy-featured man with long black hair that was now spread wildly on his forehead. I started around him on the inside, but he grabbed me and hauled me down. "I'll carry you across!" he said.

I kicked loose and fell against the wall, half dazed as my head struck rock. Fulgham was still pawing at my legs, trying to drag me back, when Charley reached down, put his hand on Fulgham's shoulder, and looked at him. Though he did no more than that, all at once Fulgham changed. Comprehension came through the mentally drained expression of drunkenness as he stared up at Charley.

Fulgham rose. "You're the only man on this whole stinking mountain, Charley!" He swung his hand in an elaborate gesture against the storm. He swayed, but Charley kept him from falling.

We found Danny on the snowy rocks on the other side of the High Place, the bottle between his knees, his head bent down. I threw the bottle down the mountain. Danny raised his head and stared at me blearily until his mind began to focus. Then he was angry. I shoved him back as he started to rise. He forgot his anger then and lay on his back, singing "The Muleskinner's Dream."

I looked around at the others. Charley made a half-turn and sat down suddenly with one leg doubled under him. His head dropped forward, and the cords of his neck showed beside the stiff ruff of his snow-caked sheepskin collar. He was laboring for breath.

"He's sick!" Fulgham shouted. "Do something for him!"

"I'm all right," Charley said. "Just a little rest . . ."

Danny sat up. "Who's sick?" He wagged his hand at Fulgham. "I said you'd get sick, didn't I?"

Fulgham staggered through the snow and grabbed me by the jacket. His coarse face was twisted, and his black hair whipped in the blast. "You can't do anything for Charley! I'm going to take him back to town!"

"A good idea," Danny said inanely. "Let's all go home." He tried to get up but fell backward.

I hit Fulgham a hard chop in the jaw. It broke his grip on me, but when he fell it was because he slipped and not because of the blow. His head cracked against a rock. As he began to rise, I kicked his legs from under him. Physically, Luke Fulgham was a brute. Alcohol, altitude and punishment, not to mention the bitter cold, were not enough to stop him.

He sat in the snow, glaring at me, ready to try again. Charley said, "We've got to go on." The simple truth of his words cut across Fulgham's anger.

Fulgham lurched up. "Get us out of here, Rhodes." For all his sodden condition, his mind had gone directly to the point. The snow was piling up. Visibility was almost gone. The cold was biting deep into us.

Charley rose. He looked like death warmed over. He pressed his left hand against his chest, hunched over as he peered at the swirling whiteness all around us. I pulled Danny to his feet and slapped his face with my stiff mitten. We all started on once more, and after a few rods I was supporting Danny and Fulgham was holding Charley upright.

Ten minutes later we were lost. I knew we were somewhere on the bench below the Queen, which had to be up to our right. Danny stumbled and dragged me down with him when he fell. The snow sliced into our faces, taking our breath away. I got Danny up and looked around, only to find both Fulgham and Charley down. Fulgham's eyes were bright as granite spalls, but blank, when I hustled him to his feet. Together we got Charley up and went on.

A half-hour later we were close to freezing. The wind was murderous. We huddled together, and Fulgham asked, accusingly, "Where are we?"

"We turn off the bench pretty soon," I said, but I didn't know where to turn. There were no cairns to mark the way; there was no definite trail from here on to the Queen.

Holding Charley with one arm, Fulgham pawed snow away from his face and stared into the storm with fear naked in his eyes. The snow coated his features again in an instant. He looked at me and mumbled, "You'd better get us there, Rhodes."

We made perhaps a hundred feet between each rest. I guessed that we had about a quarter of a mile to go before it would be time to turn off to the right. It was a bad guess, and it would have cost us our lives if it had not been for Frank Davidson's precaution.

Danny and I tripped over the rope that was stretched across the trail and held by drill steel driven into cracks in the rocks. We went to the right along the rope until we came to one of the drills. There seemed to be no other guiding line beyond the drill.

We were close to the Queen, but if we missed it we would be finished in another half-hour. I kept staring at the drill. Fulgham said, "Go on, damn you!"

"Wait till I get my bearings!" I yelled.

We wasted energy cursing each other while Danny and Charley sagged against us.

Then we heard the muffled shout not far above us.

# Chapter 2

**F**RANK DAVIDSON came lunging out of the storm and said, "Are you all right?" He dropped something he had been holding in his right hand. It fell into the snow and made a black line that disappeared quickly. It was dynamite fuse that had been tied to the drill, but the snow had covered it.

Davidson brushed past me. "I'll help Charley now," he said.

"You will like hell!" Fulgham growled.

Though I knew that he must be as close to exhaustion as I was, I saw him bend and lift old Charley across his shoulder. For a moment I stared at him stupidly, wondering at his source of strength. "Go on!" Fulgham grunted.

I dug the fuse from the snow and let my hand slide along it as we made the next lift toward the Queen.

There at the next drill, nailed to timbers Davidson had dragged down from the mine, was a sheet of corrugated iron he had used as a windbreak. The sheet was bellying in the wind. I could see where Davidson had been huddled, waiting, because the snow had not yet curled around the ends of the windbreak to fill the depression he had left.

Another line of fuse led to another drill set in the

rocks. We zigzagged on up to the timber yard of the mine. Though the cabin was only twenty feet away, we couldn't see it. Fulgham came up the last few steps to level ground. Davidson was behind him, shoving, steadying, but it was still Fulgham who bore the dead weight of old Charley.

No matter what kind of brute he was, Luke Fulgham was also a man. There were times during the winter when, in the heat generated by impacted opinion rubbing against raw feeling, I was to deny that fact.

He stood with his feet wide-placed, taking in the icy air with great gasps. "Where's the cabin?"

"Straight ahead," Danny said. "Come on."

I said, "Don't stay in the heat, you fools!" But they didn't hear me, or else they didn't care. They were safe. Let them get sick from the sudden change of temperature. Damn them anyway; it would do them good.

I felt my way out across the timber yard until my feet struck the track from the mine. Turning right with the track as a guide, I came to where I thought the blacksmith shop should be. I stepped toward it and bumped against a cornering of the logs. It is a measure of the confusion that a blinding storm creates that I went clear around the shop, guiding on the logs, until I found the door, instead of taking two steps to the right after I managed to find the first corner.

Davidson was right behind me. "Craig, I've got to explain something."

I wanted to get out of the wind, to have a chance to begin thawing gradually before I went into the heat of the cabin. I fumbled the shop door open, but it got away from me when the wind took it. Except for Davidson, it would have been ripped from its hinges.

Looking me straight in the face was a hairy gray burro. "What the hell!"

I stepped into the stout shelter, and it was like walking into another world. The wind was rocketing past the doorway, fluffing the long hair on the burro's sides, but there was no real force of it inside the building.

Davidson struggled until he pulled the door shut. I remember thinking, *The hinges have got to be moved to the other side.*

I pulled off my mittens and put my hands on the burro's shaggy side. Without the wind, the shop seemed warm. I ducked my head against the animal and wiped the snow from my face. "Any white spots, Frank?"

Davidson took his time examining me. Once or twice he touched my cheeks with his finger. He shook his head. "I got to explain something, Craig."

"Let me work some of the frost out of my joints first." I began to stamp my feet and swing my arms. The burro stood patiently. It was old Major, one of Burris's most gentle, dependable donkeys that he hired out when someone wanted to make a high ride. Not wanting to walk to the Queen, Davidson had hired the burro. He was feeling guilty about his laziness now. I expected he would take a half-hour explaining.

Davidson was a worrier. He was always so loyal to his employer's interests in every detail that he was known as a company man. He was heavy set, a man who could outlast two average muckers by holding a steady pace. His eyes were dark green, bedded so deeply beneath heavy brows that they appeared to be peering out from small caves. His hair was a pale orange color, wiry almost to the point of kinkiness, and he wore it cropped short.

He was about twenty-four, but we had always considered him much older. When he was sixteen we young brats used to poke fun at him and consider him a dolt because he continued to help his mother around her boardinghouse instead of getting a job in the mines. He was her only child. She was a tall, gaunt widow who was always saying how much better things had been before her husband decided to go west and die of tuberculosis. She would put it as if he had made both decisions simultaneously, with malice aforethought. Frank hadn't escaped the boardinghouse until he was almost twenty. Then he learned mining the way he did everything else, thoroughly and slowly.

Why the devil Lenore Enderly had married him none of us could understand. For three summers she had worked at Mrs. Davidson's boarding-house. During the winters she attended the Methodist Academy down in the valley. Every young buck in Colorow, and many of the old goats, too, had made a try for Lenore Enderly. She had been pretty thick with Danny for a while this summer, and then suddenly she had married Davidson.

We liked Frank, and we respected his skill as a miner, but he was not the kind of man to sit in on all-night poker games with you at Mack's or the Sylvanite Palace, or to go on a glorious drunk. He worked steadily, saved his money, and went home to the boardinghouse at night.

Once, when Frank was working graveyard at the Black Hawk, Viv Bonner and Teddy Weyand came to the dry-room when Davidson and some others were eating lunch. Vic and Teddy wanted a box of dynamite to blow up the cabin where a Pinkerton man was living. The Pinkerton man, who pretended to be a writer gathering material on mining towns, was really ferreting out all the assay shops in Colorow where miners sold highgrade. It was agreed that a sky-ride with a box of dynamite would settle his hash for him.

Vic and Teddy knew that the Black Hawk was the logical place to get the dynamite because the owner never knew or cared about how much powder he had on hand. Though they didn't say why they wanted the explosives, everyone guessed, of course. All the graveyard men at the Hawk were in favor of giving the box to them, but not Davidson.

It was not that he was against blowing up the Pinkerton man; he was just not going to let anyone remove anything from a mine where he was a trusted employee.

Vic and Teddy had to get the dynamite elsewhere, and almost got caught.

As soon as the shop began to feel cool—it must have been ten degrees below zero—I knew my body was warming up. I could take a chance on going into the heated cabin. Old Charley would need care, and Fulgham and Danny weren't going to be in any shape to give it.

"Don't worry about Major, Frank. Tomorrow we'll take him down past the High Place, and he'll go home in a rush."

"It ain't that that I was going to tell you."

Davidson could make any petty problem sound like a crisis, and he never could get to a point without staring at you as if you were going to beat him for something he had done. He acted as if he had been born feeling guilty.

"All right, what is it?" I said.

The storm was pounding the shop, rasping across the tin roof, banging the door back and forth across the slight leeway in the catch. I hadn't had time during the summer to weight the shop roof down with boards and rocks the way the cabin roof was secured. I worried about it while waiting for Davidson to get to his point.

He was still giving me his long, deep stare and rubbing his lips together when something bumped against the door. Major's floppy ears swung forward. The door latch lifted and someone opened the barrier a few inches. "Frank!" It was a woman's voice.

Davidson leaped to the latch and grabbed the forge-wrought grip. His wife came inside. The anger in the wind increased to a hoarse whistle as Davidson squeezed the door shut against it.

# Chapter 3

OVER her head Lenore Enderly Davidson had a jumper from the stock of clothing in the cabin. Her face was ruddy from the cold. When she threw the jumper back, I saw the sparkle of snow where it had driven up under the covering and lodged in her black hair. She was a small woman, about five feet in height.

There was an amazing vitality about her. It came from her eyes, dark as her hair; from the eager set of her lips, from her smooth movements. Some small women remind you of birds, but Lenore gave the impression of being regal. She was a beautiful woman.

In the freezing air of the shop, with the gloom almost as thick as the murky dark outside, I stared at her and said, "What are you doing here!"

She ignored the question. "Charley is pretty sick. Danny and Mr. Fulgham both passed out. I don't know what to do about them."

I gave Davidson my rage in a long look. He saw his chance to get away and leave the explaining to someone better able to handle it than he. "I'll take care of them." For once, he spoke quickly. He went out, leaning his weight against the door to force it shut.

"It's my fault, Craig. I was going down today." Lenore looked me straight in the eyes. "We slept very late. When Frank saw the storm threatening he wouldn't let me risk going back to Colorow alone, and he was afraid to go with me because he thought the rest of you might get lost on the bench in bad weather, just as you did."

Lenore's explanation was logical enough. I thought of that sheet of corrugated iron behind which Frank Davidson had huddled in the storm. Most men, having done what he had done with the rope and fuse, would have been content to stay in the cabin. But he had stayed outside, and quite likely he had saved our lives. "You had no business talking him into letting you come up here. Damn it, Lenore—"

"I know it." Lenore put her hands on Major's neck and rubbed gently. "I was ready to go to the valley the same day Frank was to come up here, but then Danny and Mr. Fulgham got into their trouble. I knew it would be a few days before you could get everything straightened out. The weather was wonderful, and I saw a chance to spend another day or two with Frank."

"Why didn't you spend the two extra days in Colorow, instead—"

"You know Frank. When it's time to go to a job, nothing holds him back."

That was Davidson, all right, with his high sense of order and duty. There weren't many women who, under any circumstances, would have cared to ride a burro up Bulmer Peak. But Lenore was different; she liked adventure. She had walked the high tipple at the Rasputin mine. She had ridden in a tram bucket to the New York, where the cable spans swayed high above a plunging gulch. And once she and Bonnie Bannerman had charmed a shift boss into letting them go all the way from the sixth level of the Royal Tiger to Zero Level fifteen hundred feet up the mountain. Underground.

It meant climbing ladders up raises that were no longer in use, going along old drifts that were caving. They actually reached Number Four Level before Fred Bannerman's superintendent caught them and sent them packing down the mountain.

Lenore had thought nothing of coming to the Queen. She probably considered it a jolly little trip. The thought of her walking across the High Place was enough to make me shudder.

"You acted like a fool, Lenore. To come up here at this time of year! My God—"

"I know it. Frank didn't want me to come, but I talked him into it. In the morning, when the storm is over, I'll take Major and leave." She flashed her own temper at me. "Just because you're the boss here is no reason for you to act like a tyrant. We all make mistakes."

"Yeah. I know." I began to feel the bitter cold of the shop. It was time to go to the cabin. "Let's get out of here," I said.

We felt our way to the track and followed it until we heard the rattling of the cabin roof close by. I do take credit for having the door facing downwind. We fell inside. The heat, light, and sudden disappearance of the pressure of the wind made an overwhelming change that, ordinarily, would have been blessed. But today one problem was dissolving into another.

Charley was in bad shape. He was in a bunk but he wanted to get out and sit in a chair. Davidson was holding him down, trying to argue with him. "I've got to sit up," Charley gasped. "Let me up."

"It's not good for you," Davidson said.

Fulgham was lying on the floor by the stove. Danny was at the table, his arms outstretched, his face mashed down against the planks. Both he and Fulgham were unconscious. Going from the door to Charley's bunk, I felt the stunning heat of the room. It was hot enough to knock anyone out.

"I'll see about him," I said to Davidson. "Drag Fulgham and Danny over by the door and open it."

"He doesn't want to stay in bed," Davidson said.

Lenore opened the door. I felt the cold draft of outside air rush along the dirt floor. Charley said, "I've got to get up and sit in a chair, I tell you!"

Davidson knocked a bench over as he got his hands under Danny's arms and dragged him to the doorway. He went back and did the same for Fulgham.

Lenore came over to me and looked at Charley.

After a while she said, "I think you'd better let him sit up, as he says."

Charley nodded. He looked as if he were dying of suffocation. After I helped him from the bunk, as he sat in a chair, holding his head up with effort. Almost instantly he seemed to be breathing better.

The big boardinghouse range, which had come over the High Place piece by piece, was showing red on top. I took off my coat, but that still wasn't enough. I was sick when I staggered to the door and stood spraddle-legged over Fulgham to lean into the air outside. The coldness was like a miracle as it drove the dizziness away.

Lenore was rubbing Charley's wrists. He was still having a time of it, but it was evident that he had known what he was talking about when he said he had to sit up. Fulgham and Danny began to stir, gulping and swallowing noisily. I looked down at them and felt like kicking them both out into the storm. Davidson was stoking more coal into the stove. We had plenty of it. The cost of it and the packing charges had made Joe Delaverne turn green.

Danny stirred a little more vigorously. He half opened his eyes and said, "What time is it?"

"Time to go to work," I said. "Get up."

He sat up and stared around him dazedly. Then he saw Lenore, and grinned. The cold against his back made him shiver. He cast a belligerent glance over his shoulder. "I froze enough for one day. Shut the door!"

"Stay right where you are until you freeze some sense into your skull."

"The big boss, huh?" Danny cocked one eye at me and grinned.

People said we looked alike, Danny and I. We had the same big frames, the same bristly sandy hair, the same stubborn Scotch-gray eyes—a general resemblance over all; but the similarity ended there. Danny didn't give a hoot for anything; I was saddled to ambition. People, especially women, liked Danny better than they liked me; there is a coldness in ambition that seeps through no matter how you try to cover it. If I spent ten dollars for drinks, among those who drank was someone who knew I had a selfish purpose in mind. If Danny bought the drinks, no one questioned the fact that he did so because he wanted to, and that was all there was to it. When Danny took a girl to a dance, there were a few basic reasons for it. When I did so, the basic reasons might be there, true; but it was also likely that someone in her background—father, uncle or cousin—was in a position to help Craig Rhodes along.

Ten years ago, when the roof caved in on the second level of the Shiloh Extension, our father was one of the six miners carried out in pieces four days later. We had a younger brother and two sisters. After a year Mother married again. It was the wisest course she could have taken, but Danny and I considered it, somehow, as a betrayal. We liked our stepfather as a man, but not as a replacement of our father.

Our mother moved away from Colorow with the rest of the family, but Danny and I stayed. Thanks to people like Ma Riley, Fred Bannerman, and Gubby O'Toole, with special thanks to Charley Spence, we grew up to be halfway decent citizens. Ma Riley and O'Toole kicked our rear ends solidly when we tried to hook out of school to pick up easy bucks kids could make running messages around town for the madams and gamblers of Southside.

Charley saw that we had a place to live. He herded us to church regularly—it didn't make any difference what church. Fred Bannerman made us work. He owned ore wagons and teams, as well as mines and warehouses. We worked long hours forking manure after school. Later, we swamped on one of his wagons, two kids doing the work of one man. Some men would have expected one kid to do it. At fifteen we went into the mines.

Danny and I grew up close together. We fought all comers. Between times we fought each other. We were close but we were not alike.

Danny lay on the floor, grinning at me, and grinning at the whole messed-up trip to the Queen. I was scowling, wearing my responsibility

34

heavily; but after a while, looking at Danny and remembering much, I had to grin too. But I wiped the smile off before the others in the room could see it.

"Wake Fulgham up," I told Danny. "I've a mind to put you two to work in the mine the rest of the day."

Fulgham was already rolling around in protest against the cold.

"Sure," Danny said. "If I had a bottle of whisky to wave under his nose, he'd come up a-snorting." He began to shake Fulgham. "Get up, you bum! They're taking us to jail again!"

I turned away and looked toward Charley. Lenore was making him comfortable. I listened to the claws of the blizzard scraping at the roof. What if she was marooned here for two or three days? Or a week? She looked at me over her shoulder. My thoughts ran away from me. Suppose just the two of us were stuck in a place like this all winter? It was easy to push aside, at least mentally, all other men when you were looking at Lenore Davidson.

"It's four o'clock," Davidson said, putting his watch away. He lifted the teakettle to make sure that it wasn't boiling dry. "Should I go down and get that fuse out of the snow tonight, Craig?"

"Lord, no!" I said. He's worrying again, I thought. I gave Lenore a quick glance. She was unlacing Charley's boots. I thought I saw a disturbed look in his expression as he watched me.

Fulgham got his neck off the doorsill and sat up. After a moment or two he seemed healthier. "When do we eat?"

"Let's go over to the Bon Ton," Danny said, "where that waitress always gives me the best of everything." He reached behind Fulgham, scooped up snow from outside, and dumped it down the collar of Fulgham's shirt. Fulgham howled. They both got up laughing. As Fulgham's eyes wandered around the room, they caught and held my sour expression for an instant, but he went right on laughing.

He and Danny were going to work tomorrow, ten hours of it. Maybe that would help take some of the high life out of them.

Fulgham walked over and leaned across the table, looking at Charley. His voice was gentle as he asked, "How you doing there, boy?"

"Oh, fine." Charley gave Fulgham a faint grin.

A little later I closed the door, and the six of us were held tightly in that big cabin. The interior was twenty by thirty feet. The floor was the natural rock of the mountain, smoothed over with earth the jack-whacker had packed up from Coney Hollow. The rafters were good red spruce three-by-twelves from a sawmill on Lion Creek. Inside, they were sealed with canvas. On the outside the heavily weighted corrugated iron roofing was overlapped and nailed securely. Still, the force of

36

the wind lifted the ends of some of the boards the rocks were laid on. When a particularly hard blast thundered across the roof, the ends of the boards would rise; then, when the wind relented a trifle, they fell back into place with a thump.

You could feel the vibration of the walls, too. The logs were the largest burros could bring up. Although they were short—no burro could have handled a full-run log for any wall—both ends of the splices were doweled with tight-fitting pins in auger holes. I had known there was wind up here, but not such wind as there was tonight. You could put your hand against any wall and feel it trembling.

One side of the cabin was set against the mountain, and on that side was an eight-by-ten storeroom dug into the rock and lined with boards. It held most of our food and a small stock of clothing and other items that I dignified as commissary goods.

We had five single bunks, two on one wall and three on the opposite wall. Against the west end was the big range, without the customary smoke hood; a half-ton of coal from the pile outside, stacked in sacks; the cupboards, a wash bench, kindling, and a round shallow fifty-gallon tank for water storage. There was water inside the Creole Queen and a good spring outside; but because the spring was frozen now, and because we didn't trust the mine water, we would be melting snow in a copper-bottomed wash boiler from now on.

Down the middle of the room was a big plank table with benches on both sides. The room was big enough for five men and more, but it would shrink before the winter was over. One woman, even for a short time, made it too small.

Danny and Fulgham found a stew on the stove, coffee in the big pot, and biscuits in the warming oven. They tossed tinware on the table and began to help themselves. Danny said: "This is fine, Lenore. Why don't you stay all winter and cook for us?"

His joke didn't come off well. Fulgham gave him a quick sidewise glance and grinned. Lenore ignored them. Standing by the platform that held the storage tank, Davidson gave my brother slow scrutiny, and then with equal deliberateness looked at his wife.

There were never any surface marks of emotion on Davidson's face. Even as a kid he had been that way. But I knew that his mind had a way of meshing evenly. Some people thought him thick-witted. He was not.

Davidson said, "I'll get that fuse first thing in the morning, Craig." He spoke as if he had been studying the problem for a long time and had arrived at the only logical solution.

After Danny and Fulgham had mopped up their plates, Fulgham dug a cigar from his shirt pocket. It was shattered but he and Danny divided it, licked the peeling wrapper into place, and sat back smoking like young princes of Bulmer Peak.

I could see that they were getting drowsy. Relaxation took some of the coarseness from Fulgham's features. As far as I noticed, Lenore never glanced at either of them. In fact, she was too obviously unaware of them.

After a while I blew out the lamps and told Danny and Fulgham to go to bed. They stumbled around as they undressed. Fulgham said, "Well, what do you know—a mattress and real springs!"

"The best of everything," Danny said. "I wish I was back in jail on the Southside."

They were asleep shortly after I relit the lamps.

Lenore's dark, expressive eyes met mine. "I'll stay here with Charley," she said.

"So will I."

"You may as well go on to bed if you want to," Lenore told her husband.

He looked at his watch. "A quarter after six. I guess I may as well."

Though the time was just a few minutes after dark, it had been dark since we left timberline. It seemed like midnight now. Davidson stripped down to his long underwear and got into bed. A few minutes later he rose to put more coal in the stove. Danny and Fulgham were snoring like fat bears. The wind kept slapping boards up and down, and I knew that the motion must be working some of the rocks off them.

I got out my time book. I was supposed to keep a log for Delaverne of all developments in the mine. The book was the dues ledger of the Mountain Knights, a lodge that had flourished briefly in Colorow, until the brethren discovered that the ritual was not well suited to their strenuous way of life, and that the main purpose of the lodge was to sell insurance to the members. As the first and last secretary-treasurer of this mystic group, I had retained the ledger. The "altar" I had given to Kansas Nellie because she was always complaining that she had nothing real tony on which to display her potted geraniums.

The geraniums and the altar were busted up together when the cribbing of the settling pond at the Eclipse Mill gave way one morning—but that's another story.

I set down the date boldly, *Oct. 26, 1888,* and then I didn't know what to say. I considered, *Arrived at the Creole Queen safely.* That sounded like bravado, and the word *arrived* seemed to be high-flown. My first entry in the log read:

*Oct. 26, 1888—Got here. Storming.*

Lenore kept giving Charley hot coffee. Second-guessing the kind of heart trouble he had, it's a wonder that the wind on the trip up didn't kill him, or that Davidson, first, and later I, didn't kill him

40

by keeping him lying down when he should have been sitting.

"Charley, you'd better go down as soon as you can make it," I said. "You can send me up another man."

Charley shook his head. "I'll be all right by tomorrow afternoon. These spells don't come very often."

Though Lenore agreed with me, we couldn't change Charley's mind. I had the feeling that we were arguing with a man who could see beyond the petty details of the moment, and who understood human beings much better than they knew themselves.

He kept shaking his head at us, smiling. "I'm needed here about as much as any place."

I glanced at Davidson. He seemed to be asleep. "Frank can take you down tomorrow, Lenore. There'll be no need for him to come back."

Lenore nodded. "I didn't want him to come up here in the first place."

I took it as an admission that affairs between her and Danny had been as strong as Delaverne had suspected. "Why'd you marry him?" I asked, in a low voice.

She hesitated a moment, then: "He has a calmness that I need greatly."

Charley was watching me with a quiet, almost priestly, expression.

After a while I grew drowsy, and then fell asleep

at the table with my head on my arms. I was roused suddenly by a tearing sound that came faintly above the wind. The roof was being torn off the blacksmith shop.

I yelled at Danny and Fulgham and Davidson. The latter came out of his bunk so quickly that I knew he had not been asleep. Fulgham responded next but I had to shake Danny and drag him part way out of the bunk before he woke up.

We left him staggering around as he dressed. Fulgham and Davidson and I went out. In utter darkness the storm was a furry, howling thing. "Get timbers from the yard!" I yelled.

I groped my way over to the shop and kept shouting to guide the others. From the high bank at the back of the shop I felt along the roof. Some sheets of corrugated iron were already gone, ripped from the nails, leaving curled strips of metal that tore my hands. The whole roof was drumming. One sheet was flapping with such force that it could slash a man's arm or face.

Fulgham and Davidson followed my shouts. We heard Danny yelling, and I told him what to do. We got one timber on the roof, and Danny and Fulgham stumbled away after another.

"Bring a log over here!" I yelled at Danny.

I went around the corner of the building to make myself better heard. Danny came rushing through the night with an eight-foot timber.

The end took me squarely in the belly and

knocked all interest out of me. It hurled me on my back in the snow on top of the track. And there I lay, striving mightily to get breath that seemed gone forever.

Danny didn't even know he'd struck me.

The three of them went on fighting the storm and the flapping tin until the roof was weighted down. Then one of them thought to inquire, "Where the hell did Craig go all of a sudden?"

I was still alive, but doubled over, with my rear to the wind, and grateful that no one could see me. "Over here," I said. "Did you get it fixed?"

"Any more timber would cave it in," Danny replied. "If this is the kind of work you expect all winter, I'm going down the hill tomorrow."

"You'd like that trip, wouldn't you?" Fulgham said, and laughed.

Davidson said nothing.

We found our way back to the cabin. While the others were crowding in, I tried to straighten up entirely. There is enormous indignity about being lanced in the belly with a ten-inch log. It was nobody's business. But Danny saw me holding my stomach and trying to stand as if nothing had happened.

It came to him clearly. "I *thought* I brushed against something with my first log! Just where did I hit you with it, Craig?"

I didn't get my hands away before Fulgham noticed. He and Danny began to roar. They kept on laughing at my sick expression while they hunted up a snack. They were chuckling when they got in bed again; and then they were snoring like contented hogs.

Tomorrow. Tomorrow, I thought, we'll have some organization around this place.

# Chapter 4

I CAME AWAKE into one of the rare voids that occurred during the winter when there was no wind. The room was warm. One of the lamps was burning on the table. I thrust my head out of the bunk and saw Charley reading beside the light.

Without looking at me he said, "Good morning, Craig."

His face was tired. His gray whiskers seemed to have sprouted half an inch in the last day and night. "Don't you think you ought to go down, Charley?"

"I see no reason to go down."

"You could send up another man," I said, even though it was unlikely that anyone would want to come to the Queen now.

"Unless you want to get rid of me, I'd rather stay."

I got up and dressed. Fulgham and Danny were still sleeping. Davidson was lying with his eyes open. His inscrutability was already worrying me. What would it be like if he stayed? I had made a bad error by letting him come to the Queen. He did not look at me as I watched him.

I began to wonder if he ever slept like other men.

Lenore was in Charley's bunk, curled on her

side. She was under blankets, but I saw the top of her woolen dress and knew that she was clothed.

"She was tired," Charley said.

I looked at a rumpled pile of blankets shoved to one end of the table. "You slept there?"

"A little. I was comfortable."

Davidson swung out and sat on the edge of his bunk. "I'll have to take Lenore down, if it ain't too bad outside. Is there anything—"

"I wouldn't ask any man to come back up that trail," I said. "You stay down, Frank."

Davidson rubbed his hand across his wiry red hair. "You asked Charley to send a man up, when you asked him if he was going down."

"I've changed my mind."

Davidson thought a while. "On snowshoes—"

"Webs or not, stay down once you're there."

Davidson looked slowly across at Danny's bunk. It might have been accidental, since he followed up with a slow look all around the room. Accidental or not, Davidson was one mistake I was glad I was correcting.

I started outside. Snow was curled in a fine tracery inside on the sill. The door was hard to open. I stepped out into snow well above my knees. More snow was falling. Before I shut the door I called back to Charley: "Get everybody up! We've got to move fast!"

The snow made a yielding softness against my legs as I pushed out to the timber yard and then on to look down toward the bench. It was no freakish blizzard around me, but a heavy winter storm laying down snow for all it was worth. Visibility was not as poor as yesterday because there was no wind, but there was still a heavy gloom. I could not see to the bench.

I shoved my way over to the blacksmith shop to get the burro. Major blinked at me when I got the door open. His back was covered with snow, and more snow was lying in a slanting pile over a third of the shop. I found the saddle in one corner and brushed him off carefully with the blanket before I put the saddle on.

Davidson was looking from the doorway of the cabin when I came out of the shop leading the burro. I yelled: "Don't waste time on breakfast! Get ready to go!"

He was stuffing his gear in a duffel bag when I went inside. I told him to hurry. Danny leaned out with a bleary expression from his upper bunk and said, "What's this about no breakfast?"

"Get out of there, you and Fulgham. We're taking Davidson and Lenore below the High Place."

Lenore's woolen dress looked warm enough. She had a heavy jacket. I handed her the jumper she had thrown over her head last night. "How's your shoes?" She held one foot out. She was wearing stout high button shoes of calfskin. I grabbed a gunny sack from the storeroom, ripped it in two, and told her to tie the pieces around her feet.

"If you feel all right, Charley, you can start breakfast while we're gone," I said.

He had just looked outside. "Maybe I'd better start it for all of us."

"We'll go far enough to be sure they can make it. I think Major can break his way through," I said. Major was hungry. He knew where home was. Once started, the last thing Major would do was turn back. It was all downhill, and the snow hadn't settled or hadn't been blown into hardness yet.

We took two square-point shovels. Danny and Fulgham carried them. They sat on them and tried to slide down the first incline after we left the timber yard. I said, "Stop that damned foolishness!"

Lenore rode Major, and Davidson went first, leading the burro. By the time we got down to the bench below the Queen, my worries began to lessen. We were making fair progress. The cumulative effects of pushing snow all the way to Colorow would tire out the Davidsons, but at least it looked like they wouldn't have any trouble going down.

We came to the High Place. My sore belly began to get knots in it. I turned to take a shovel from Danny, but he went around me and out on the trail. Fulgham followed him and they probed their way across, feeling under the snow for ice. Yesterday, when the wind had been raging, there had been hardly any snow on the rocky point.

Danny yelled back from the other side: "It's all right. Just hold close to the edge!"

Davidson led Major across. Lenore went behind the burro, and I came last. For some reason the crossing was not as terrifying as yesterday; still, I wasn't happy on it.

Once across, we immediately ran into drifts. Shoulder high, Davidson smashed the way through the first one. Major followed unhesitatingly, the fine snow tumbling down like white dust on his shoulders and back. On the other side was the bare rock of the mountain, cold and gray. Just beyond that another swooping drift went up, even higher than the first.

I took the lead and beat a way through. Beyond was bareness once more, and then another drift. The snow filtered through our clothes. It came down our necks and pushed up under the legs of our pants. Body heat began to melt it.

And all the while more snow was coming down in a gray pall.

Our progress was very slow. The exertion of wallowing through one drift after another began to tell, and although we were not hurt yet, I knew that if there was as much as a half-mile of drifts we were not going to get the Davidsons through that day.

Somewhere short of Coney Hollow we came to

a bare spine, almost a knife edge of rock running up the mountain. I said, "Wait here and I'll go up and see if I can get a look ahead." A gust of wind came against me as I started, knocking a thin wave of snow up and over the spine, like smoke racing close to the ground.

I climbed until I came to overhanging snowbanks caught in the higher rocks. The mountain, I knew without being able to see, was sheer above me.

Intermittent at first, the wind was beginning to build up its steady force once more. I could see into Coney Hollow, and all the way to it lay wave after wave of drifts. A frozen ocean of them, with the crests just beginning to throw spindrift before the wind.

The unpredictable currents of the wind had built those drifts on the east side of the High Place, but perhaps if we could get beyond Coney Hollow . . .

The frozen breakers of snow were there, going on and on. And then the wind came in again and cut my vision off. There had been an awesome beauty in the sight. It held me after I could no longer see beyond Coney Hollow. Crest after crest of pure whiteness swept up in bold, haunting lines, a tracery of beauty that was both delicate and startling.

Danny yelled at me from below. The intelligibility of the words was swept away, but his tone carried impatience.

Puffs of white rolled up toward the rocky spine and broke and streamed away with the growing wind.

"Well?" Fulgham said when I returned. He had led the way through two more drifts.

"It's blocked like this for as far as I could see."

"That wasn't far." Fulgham began to smash his shovel into the next drift.

"Forget it," I said. "We haven't a chance to get out of here today."

"We won't get anywhere standing here jawing!" Fulgham went on with his efforts.

I shook my head at Lenore. "It's like this for the best part of a mile, I'd say. The wind changed and let me get a fair look."

Lenore nodded. "We go back, then."

"We'll have to wait the storm out, and then you can get down," I told Lenore. But I was afraid. Two inches of snow had piled up on Major's rump while we were arguing.

We started back, but Major would not come. He knew the way home; he was not going back to the mine where there was nothing for him to eat. When I took the saddle and bridle off and threw them aside, Lenore protested.

"We can't feed him," I said. "His only chance is to work his way down."

"We could feed him for a day or two," Lenore said.

We left the burro and started back. Major looked

over his shoulder at us, and then walked slowly toward the drift in front of him.

All told, our futile trip took four hours. The storm was growing worse by the time we reached the mine. After eating, I took Danny and Fulgham and Davidson outside to repair the roof of the shop. Sometimes it took all four of us to handle the sheets against the wind.

When the roof was repaired I sent Danny and Fulgham into the breast to drill and put Davidson to work shooting out a timber station not far from the portal. Charley was in the shop when I returned to it.

"They'll miss her at the Academy," I said. "They'll start inquiring around, and before we know it somebody will come up on webs and—"

"I don't think so. I've been talking to her, Craig. She didn't intend to go back to the Academy anyway, after she was married, not until Davidson got this job up here. They won't be expecting her back. That isn't important anyway. Nobody's going to come up this mountain after her, because when they find out they'll know she's with her husband. She did a foolish thing, but it will look to others like it was deliberate. No one down below is going to worry one bit about her."

"I'll build some snowshoes for her and Davidson. There's some way to get them down."

"I hope so," Charley said.

"You're not trying to say she's stuck here for the winter? My God, Charley! If—"

"Would you start off here, after today, with your wife on homemade snowshoes?"

"If I had a wife, I wouldn't let her talk me into getting in a fix like this in the first place." That was no answer, I knew. "You mean Davidson won't let her try it?"

"I doubt it, Craig. It would take a strong man, used to snowshoes, to go down this mountain. Davidson knows that."

"She can't stay here!"

"Where's she going?" Charley asked gently.

"We'll see."

Though it was only the second day, it seemed that the storm had been going on for weeks. I went down to the bench and dragged the rope from the snow. Coiled around my shoulders it was not a great weight, yet it was all I wanted to carry through the deepening snow. The force of the wind was as strong as that of yesterday, but it was not nearly so cold.

Without stopping to warm up, I went back and got the fuse, throwing it in big coils to keep from breaking the stiff, tarry covering. Charley had cleaned up the shop and put things in order. We hung the loose, rattling coils of fuse on nails overhead and built up the fire.

"Where they going to sleep?" Charley asked.

I had thought of the shop, but it was a drafty

place and it was crowded with sacks of forge coal and other supplies that could not be put outside. I had thought, also, of widening one of the bunks in the cabin some way, but that was no good either.

"We'll have to move the stuff out of the storeroom and fix up the bridal chamber there," I said.

"I'll go help her do that," Charley said, and I knew that he had thought of the storeroom before I had, but had waited for me to make the decision.

When he tried to close the shop door against the wind, I had to leap to help him. Charley was not as well as he thought he was. I remembered when Danny and I had seen him lift a sixteen-pound hammer by holding the extreme end of the handle and using only wrist and forearm power.

The fuse made black stains on my hand as I sat by the stove and ran it into rolls small enough to store handily.

Davidson came in to get more steel. He looked at the fuse for a time and said, "Did you get the drills too?"

"No!" A half dozen drills out there under the snow. We had plenty of steel; we could recover the drills next summer.

Davidson was surprised at my curtness. He stood for a while like a big child who has been rebuffed. It was easy to underestimate the man, to think him thick-headed. I made that mistake over and over, knowing better all the time.

"We ought to run a wire from the portal to some place close to the cabin," he said. "On days like this we could hold onto it and use it as a guide."

It was a good idea. I wondered how long he had been figuring it out. Just outside the mine portal was a sharp crease in the mountain. With waste from the tunnel we had filled the upper part of the channel only enough to lay track across it. On a murky day like this a man could miss the crossing and take a nasty fall about fifteen feet straight down the mountain.

"We'll do that when it clears up," I said.

Davidson started to leave with his steel.

"Frank, we've got to figure some way to get Lenore down from here."

He thought it over. "Yeah, I know."

"I can rig up a couple of pair of webs, I think, something that will work well enough for you and her to get down."

"I don't know, Craig. I'd have to see the webs first before I'd want her to take the chance."

"It's no good to have her here very long. You know that as well as I do."

Davidson gave me a steady look. "It's unhandy, her being here, but I don't see nothing bad coming from it."

He went out. I noticed how easily he closed the door with one hand.

When the fuse was rolled, I went into the mine. As I groped my way through the storm to the heavy wind door at the portal, Davidson's idea about the wire made practical sense. With the wind door shut, all outside worries seemed to be cut off. It's like that underground if you know what you're doing; if you carry your worries inside, you may not live long. I don't mean that the Creole Queen was a dangerous hole; it was not developed enough to be dangerous yet.

We were in only a hundred feet. There were two sets of timbers at the portal, and after that the rest was solid rock that needed no support.

Candlesticks were stabbed into the lagging of the second set of timbers. Picture a pencil with a loop bent into one end for a handle, the other end coming down from four sides to a sharp point. In the middle, sticking out from the slender run of steel like a bracket, is a clip to hold the candle, and opposite the clip rises a sharp, curving hook. You can jab the sharp end of the candlestick into a crevice or you can hang it by the curving hook on a rocky wall while you're working.

I lit the candle away from the draft at the door and went on into the even warmth of the tunnel. The candle threw dull orange light and made my shadow a hulking, flickering thing on the damp walls.

Davidson was drilling to shoot out the timber station. I watched him for a moment. With a single jack he could beat me by four inches on a three-foot hole. He was a powerful man, but it was the steady, even pounding that made him an expert driller.

I went on in to the breast where Danny and Fulgham were working. They stopped when they heard me coming. They were talking about women when I got there. Some men can't talk about women without being filthy and disgusting. My opinion of Fulgham had told me that was the way it would be with him; but it was not.

I listened to their talk for a while and was surprised to discover that there were sides to my brother's thinking that I had not known, and to realize that Fulgham was not exactly the kind of roughneck boomer I had taken him to be.

In the meantime I did not overlook the placement of the hole they were drilling, or the length of the last drill they had run down. They had not been loafing.

"Where's Lenore going to sleep?" Danny asked.

"Let me worry about that. She's not going to be here all winter, you know."

"You think not?" Danny said, grinning.

"Just drive this tunnel into the hill, boys. I'll worry about other details."

They grinned at each other. With Danny, it was a way of poking fun at my stuffiness. I could take it from him, but I always read into any smile of Fulgham's a deep, basic dislike of myself. They went back to work, Danny striking with the double jack, Fulgham turning the steel.

Outside, the storm was again an explosive force. I bent into it and forced my way to the cabin.

Charley and Lenore had dragged the supplies out of the storeroom and moved Davidson's mattress and springs in there on the floor.

"Leave those sacks of potatoes in there if you can find room," I said irritably, "or some night they'll freeze."

"We intended to put them back," Charley said. His look was an appeal for me to keep my temper and make the best of a bad situation.

The door of the storeroom was built in three sawdust-filled sections, ledged down to meet the terraces of the jamb in a snug fit that made the storeroom almost air-tight. There was no catch inside, only a wooden button to hold the door shut from the outside. While I watched, Charley made a slit in one end of a leather strap, nailed the other end to the door, and drove a nail beside the jamb so that the door could be lightly held from the inside.

There was a small vent through the planks and earth of the roof, but the door would have to be left part way open in order to allow ventilation for human beings.

I kept staring at the narrow bed, at Lenore's small, trim figure as she moved around. I thought of her husband with that orange-red, wiry hair, deep-set eyes, and sure, slow movements in everything he did. I wondered again why she had married him. Calmness. In a pig's left eye!

I went back to the shop as quickly as I could.

That night after supper I made the second entry in the log.

*Oct. 27—Working half a shift.*

# Chapter 5

THE SOUND that woke me in the night was something that I had been expecting. As I lay there listening to the snow driving across the corrugations of the roof, I knew, also, that I had been worrying about my personal reaction to a situation that had been bound to come.

It was not the wind that had wakened me, but the soft shutting of the storeroom door. It could not have been much of a noise, but it had brought me wide awake.

The vault-like door could shut off all sounds of what was going on beyond it but it could not still imagination; and at night imagination is a sharp, unfettered thing.

There was no doubt that Fulgham and Danny were sleeping as luxuriously as cats. Old Charley—you could not tell about him. His sleep was always light, and any small sound could waken him.

The wind growled against the edges of the sheet-iron roof. We had placed more rocks on top. The wind was not going to get our roof, but it kept prowling, humming at every tiny looseness, searching ceaselessly for weakness. The cabin logs creaked and groaned, adjusting themselves under the heavy hand of winter.

I lay tensely, hearing and seeing what I could not hear or see beyond the storeroom door.

Sometime later the storeroom door was opened a little. It was carefully done. The hinges were new; they made no great noise. But the wind and all the other night noises of the frozen mountain could not conceal the sound of the door. A minute or two later I heard someone going back to bed, quietly.

It was Lenore, of course. Davidson would have made four times as much noise. Not long afterward I heard him snoring gently. I heard Charley turn over. He too had been awake and listening.

Sleep was coming at last when I heard the wind-torn cry from somewhere outside. Then it was gone, and it could not have been anything more than the wind twisting something loose in the timberyard or at the shop. But the sound came once more, a lonely, desperate call from something living.

The storm raised its own voice in the blackness of the mountain, as if peering at any living thing that dared to be upon Bulmer Peak in winter. Again I heard the noise; and then I knew what it was.

Lenore was already out of bed, crying: "Craig! Major is out there! He's come back!"

Davidson was grunting sleepily. I got out of my bunk and began to dress, silently cursing Lenore for bringing the burro to the Creole Queen.

Charley was up too. He said: "Never mind, Lenore. Craig and me will get him."

In the fury of slashing snow that seemed to gloat because warm things had been driven from their burrow, I found my way to the edge of the timberyard and yelled downhill, "Major!"

Lenore came out of the night and bumped against me. "We've got to get him up here!"

"What for?" I was savage. The snow was up to my thighs. "If he's down there on the bench we can't risk going after him just to kill him. That's all we can do for him now, wherever he is."

"No!" Lenore said.

I took her by the shoulders to shake sense into her. Everything was her fault anyway, and now she was being a fool. A hand pressed my forearm gently and Charley said: "He's right, Lenore. We've got nothing here to feed him." His calmness rebuked both of us.

I took my hands from Lenore's shoulders. Her voice was normal when she spoke. "Can't we find out how close he is? Let's not desert him if we can help it."

I called the burro's name again.

We heard the lonesome, haunting answer.

A man came floundering through the snow. "I've got the rope. If we go more than a hundred feet, I'll have to unroll the fuses too." It was Davidson, of course.

We heard the bray again. Major was not too far down the hill. "Give me one end of the rope," I said. My first two steps off the dump threw me headfirst into the snow, and I had to struggle to rise. At the end of the rope I stopped and yelled at Major. He brayed his answer, somewhere over to the left and farther down the mountain than I had thought.

It was folly going after him. Saving him just to kill him.

I let go of the rope and went on down. I found him deep in the snow, with snow drifted against him. His coat was icy and his head was down. He made no response when I tried to urge him up the hill.

They were yelling on the dump. Only fragments of words came to me, but I gathered they were trying to tell me I had gone beyond the rope. My heavy clasp knife was hard to fumble open with freezing fingers. My left hand felt along Major's cheek and up to his neck. Under the ice and snow on his back was a cross, the cross that legend says came to all burros because one carried Christ.

Major stood as if already frozen. After several moments I put the knife away and yelled angrily: "Come down here! God damn you, come down here and help me!"

They came, Charley and Davidson, shouting to know the way, guided by my angry answers. Touched by light one moment, a man is a black, profane creature a moment later. I could not kill Major, but I could, an instant later, curse all men because I thought I had been weak.

We got the burro to the mine by dint of shouts and blows and sheer brute force. Lenore came tumbling down to help us the last half of the way. We took Major into the cabin. He stood with his head down, iced to the ears. I kept wondering why I had gone out to save him.

Charley was building up the fire. Lenore said, "I'll make him some pancakes. He hasn't had anything to eat since the oats I brought ran out."

"Pancakes! Hell'safire! I should have cut his throat when I started to."

"What stopped you?" Charley looked at me as if he knew the answer to the question. He might have. It was he who had told me about the cross upon the backs of burros in the first place.

"It won't hurt to feed him, I guess," I said.

Water began to run from Major's back. Rubbing down his shaggy wet hide with gunny sacks, Charley and I looked at each other over the brown cross. The heat rose in the burro. He ate the pancakes Lenore made, and then stood drowsing in the warmth.

It was two o'clock in the morning. We went back to bed. Danny and Fulgham had slept peacefully through the whole affair.

The storm died some time before dawn. Davidson was up early, shoveling out in front of the door. We all joined him there one by one, standing with our breaths pouring vapor into the light wind. Now we could see where we were and what had happened to the mountains during the last two days and nights. Our position shrank. We became small as we looked out for a hundred miles on gleaming whiteness.

The Sangre de Cristo range, one of the sharpest in the West, was a small string of hills far away. The valley was twenty shining miles below us, as yet unbroken by a single road, with all the ranches and even the trees covered with snow so that there was an unmarked expanse of newness everywhere.

Colorow we could not see, for it lay beyond a high spur range to the southeast, only ten miles away, with its eight thousand people. To us it was as good as ten thousand miles away.

On the crests of the Flying Horse Mountains off to the southwest, some of them almost as high as Bulmer, snow pennants were flying against the sky, living streaks against the great blue sky. Light wind was scudding snow across the bench below us, playfully tossing gusts of white that rose straight up and then broke and fell in sparkling dust back to the solid body of the snowfields.

The snow was drifted against the wind door of the Queen to half the vertical run of the yellow planks. Logs in the timberyard made a white hump that blended into the mountains beyond it. In dying, the storm had draped a delicate tracery of lace on the upper halves of the brown logs of the blacksmith shop, and the wind had molded the snow on top into a lop-sided hat such as some old men in Colorow wore.

It seemed that nature had tried to hide all the ugliness of man's work. There was peace upon the world that speech would profane.

I watched Lenore's face as she looked out on the scene. Her eyes were sparkling. There was a vibrant glow on her delicately boned features, and she seemed to be holding her breath as she drank in all the silent beauty before us.

The depth of the snow on the dump, where I measured it later, was five feet. Where Lenore stood, in the trench her husband had shoveled out, her head was a foot below the piled up snow.

Danny broke the spell when he said, "It sure is a pretty sight, boys." He went back into the cabin to put his shirt on, giving Major a solid whack upon the shoulder in passing.

Davidson began to shovel a path toward the outhouse, which sat at the far end of the timberyard over Shady Groff's old prospect hole. I marveled that the building had not been blown clear into Warner Basin. On two sides of it the snow was blown away, exposing the rocks we had piled around the structure the summer before to keep it from being toppled by the wind.

Major was not disposed to venture outside. We let him stay in the cabin while Charley and Lenore cooked breakfast. I watched Lenore mixing batter for baking-powder pancakes, and right then I decided she was not much of a cook. Baking-powder pancakes! I made a note to set a batch of sourdough that very day.

No one complained about the pancakes. Even Davidson, whose mother was the best cook in Colorow, ate them as if they were the joy of his life. Major thought they were fine too.

"There's no use to feed him," I told Lenore.

She gave me a hurt look. "We could keep him a few days, couldn't we?"

"It's no use." I didn't like the situation any better than she did. "But go ahead and feed him."

Immediately after breakfast, before I had a chance to give orders, the crew skinned out of the cabin and started shoveling snow like demons. They wanted to get inside the mine in a hurry.

I made up a batch of sourdough and put it on a shelf behind the stove so that it would start working. Quite likely I did the whole thing in an insulting manner.

Lenore said: "I know I can't cook, but I'll try to learn. You don't have to be so nasty about it."

"I'm not being nasty."

"You are too. You've been hard and mean in everything you've done since you found me here."

"I've got a job to do here this winter."

"I know, and you're going to hate me every minute I'm here. I know I made a silly mistake and maybe I know how you feel, but you're making *me* feel like a criminal, Craig. Why don't you make those snowshoes today?"

"No use until the snow settles down some, and until we're sure the storms are over for a while. I'll get to it, don't worry."

"All right. In the meantime let me help as much as I can."

"Sure," I said. "The first thing you can do is keep that storeroom door open all the time. Do you want to drive everyone in this room crazy?"

There was a long silence while Lenore gave me that disturbing, searching look of hers. "I'll talk to Frank about that. I think he'll understand."

"He ought to sleep out here!"

"You'd force him to do that?"

"Yes! If you don't."

"Why, Craig?"

"I've explained it to you already! What kind of woman are you that you won't understand what I mean?"

"I think I understand."

"All right." I turned away and tried to force Major outside, but he would not go. I picked up a shovel at the door and said, "When I yell to you, get a biscuit or something and have him follow you out."

"Don't make me do that, Craig!"

"You brought him up here. He'll follow you one more time."

I shoveled as little as possible, tramping the snow down where I could to make a trench out to the extreme end of the timberyard. The others knew what I was doing and worked harder to get to the mine before I finished. They had no chance of beating me because they had to clean clear down to the track so that we could tram out the muck from yesterday's shots.

They were just past the shop when I went after a double jack, an eight-pound striking hammer. "All right, Davidson," I said.

He turned from his shoveling and looked at me, still bent over. "Oh, hell no, Craig."

"You brought him up here." I wouldn't look at Charley.

Charley came over with Davidson to the place at the west end of the timberyard. I gave Davidson the hammer and he stared at it as if it were hot. Charley said, "Craig, there's no use——"

I yelled at Lenore to decoy Major over to us. Her face was white as she came through the snow, leading the burro with the promise of a biscuit. She gave the biscuit to Major when they reached us. She put her head down on his neck a moment and then ran back to the cabin.

"All right, Frank."

Davidson let the hammer handle rest against his leg as he used both hands in a vague, protesting gesture. "I remember Major when he was a colt. I used to——"

"I remember him when he carried Christ!" I said. "Kill him."

Charley gave me a strange look. I felt the force of it, although I saw his face only from the corner of my eye.

"If we had a sixshooter or a rifle, maybe . . ." Davidson said helplessly. "But I can't . . ."

Charley took the hammer from the snow and swung it. The sound of it was proof that one blow was enough. I remember the long, warm hair on Major's belly as the wind moved it gently, and the clean, varnished look of the hoofs as they settled into the snow. I was sick with rage at myself for forcing this task on anyone, and at the same time furious because Davidson had escaped punishment.

Charley's action I could understand; it shamed me and made me small, but that did not cure my anger at Davidson.

"Gut him, Davidson," I said. "We might run short of grub before the winter is over. He'll keep right there."

"In the name of heaven, Craig—" Charley said, but I stepped past him and stood close to Davidson and forced my will on him with a wickedness of spirit that left me weak afterward.

Davidson went to work with a sick look on his face. Charley helped him. I walked away quickly and left them there. Lenore had heard it all from the cabin doorway. I glanced at her, and I have never seen since such a look of mingled hate and wonder as she gave me.

Charley and Davidson came to the shop afterward when I was dressing steel, working at it like a fiend. "If you feel all right, Charley, drill with Frank on the timber station."

Davidson took his steel and went away.

"You want her, and I can understand that," Charley said. "She knows it. What kind of winter will it be here if all the others know it too?"

"It's not that bad. I acted like I did because the two of them upset everything here. I wanted to hurt them. Now I'm sorry about it."

"There's nothing to be gained from remorse, once you've admitted its existence."

Charley went on to the mine. His words stayed with me. Many of the simple things he said had a way of rolling in my mind and developing several faces of meaning that had to be looked upon.

At noon when we went to the cabin to eat, Lenore put on my plate a piece of baked meat that puzzled me for a moment. When I recognized what it was I was too shocked to feel anger. I glanced around me. My brother and Fulgham and Davidson were eating like wolves; they had not seen what was before me.

Lenore stood with her back to the stove, meeting my look with a bitter, defiant expression.

Major's heart lay on my plate.

Charley took the plate, went to the stove, and

dumped the heart into the fire, doing it so unobtrusively that the others paid no attention. It was only when Davidson looked up by chance as he reached for something on the table that he caught the set look between Lenore and me. His face took on a puzzled expression; then all emotion receded to the deep caves of his eyes.

"Now you're even and the childishness is over," Charley said.

The bitterness hung between Lenore and me for another moment, and then, with a glance at Charley, we dropped our eyes, knowing that indeed we both had acted miserably.

A month later nothing so tense could have happened in the cabin without Danny and Fulgham observing it; but they were not yet as deeply involved in the tangled, strained emotions that were part of living at the Creole Queen as they were to be before very long.

In the log that evening I wrote:

*Oct. 28—Storm over. Tunnel heading 104 ft.*

# Chapter 6

**F**OR ABOUT TWO WEEKS there were periods of clear weather alternating with storms that increased the snow depth greatly. In the timberyard the snow was always deep, but there were bare spots around the buildings and up toward the spine of Bulmer. Sometimes the deep trench where the track ran would be drifted half full of fluffy snow; at other times the wind scoured it clear. We could never predict the vagary of the wind. We shoveled snow almost constantly, for if one of our working runways happened to be cleared by the wind, another would surely be blocked by drifts.

As Davidson had suggested, we strung a wire to guide us to the portal of the mine on bad days. It ran from a post where the track turned on the dump to a spike in a timber at the mine entrance. On snow-blind days guiding on the wire became a habit.

There were times when blowing snow so obscured vision that it was impossible to see the blacksmith shop from the track where it passed within six feet of the building. On days like that I guided myself by the slatting sound of the roof sheets in the wind.

But one afternoon I missed the shop entirely during a darkness of driving snow and started toward the crest of Bulmer Peak over a patch of bare ground.

I knew I was lost, of course. Turning one way, I blundered into a snowbank. I tried another direction and struck snow again. In spite of two failures I was still contemptuous of the storm: the stop was very close. A man was losing his grip if he couldn't find it. Once again I struck out and wound up on bare rock. The same rock where I had been? Or had I actually climbed up the mountain when I thought I was not climbing?

I was without a coat or hat because I had not expected to be out in the storm more than a few seconds. It was probably thirty degrees below zero, and the wind was a million knives.

Before I plunged away on a new tack I got hold of myself. I kicked rocks loose and began to throw them about me, listening. They made no sound of striking until I thought to arch them high, and then, when I was picturing myself a hundred yards from any building, I heard the faint rattle of one of the rocks hitting the roof of the shop. I tossed a half dozen more to be sure, and then followed the sound.

The shop had been no more than fifteen feet away from me at any time.

When I got inside I discovered that one of my earlier rocks had broken a pane in the window— and I hadn't even heard the noise. With a piece of powder box I patched the window. On the wire outside, I clamped a track bolt to mark the place to turn toward the shop on stormy days.

Fulgham came from the mine a little later and ripped his fingers on the square corners of the nut. He came into the shop cursing. "Why didn't you tell me that damned bolt was on the wire?"

"I just now put it there."

"You should have said so."

"You should have been wearing gloves."

"I don't believe in gloves, Rhodes."

He always used my last name and Danny's first name; it was a deliberate insult that was getting under my hide more each time he did it. Trouble was due between us. Storm or no storm, now was as good a time as any to lick him.

"Some fine morning, Fulgham, you'll clamp your mitt on that wire when your hand's damp and you'll leave a nice strip of your palm when you pull away."

"That's my worry, Rhodes. Why didn't you tell us you'd put that bolt out there?"

"You're looking for trouble, huh? You came to the right place."

"I doubt that, Rhodes. *Your* speed is making it tough on Lenore and her half-witted husband."

That held me for a moment. Fulgham was right. I had, with a succession of little acts and remarks, made things as unpleasant as I could for Lenore and Davidson. It was enraging, though, to have Fulgham aware of it.

"Let's go out on the dump," I said. We couldn't see much out there, but once we had a grip on each other I wasn't worried about seeing.

Fulgham was turning toward the door when Charley came in with steel on his shoulder. "Say," Charley said, "I tore my glove on your doggone bolt, Craig." He held his hand out and then he let it drop as he looked from me to Fulgham. He reached out and took Fulgham's wrist and turned the hand up.

Fulgham had a bad rip and his whole hand was bloody. "Better have Lenore put some arnica on that," Charley said. "It's all right."

Charley went on as if he hadn't heard, as if he hadn't seen the bristling tension between me and Fulgham. "I saw a man get blood poisoning from less than that. They took off his arm but he died anyway. You have Lenore fix that up, Luke."

Fulgham had been watching me all the time. When he looked at Charley, his heavy, coarse face underwent a change. His lips were thick and he had big, faintly yellowish teeth, the kind that are usually as sound as a silver dollar. There could not have been anything pretty in his smile, and yet, looking at Charley, he suddenly became a pleasant, agreeable man.

"Maybe you're right, Charley," Fulgham said. He gave me a go-to-hell glance and went out.

"He's no more afraid of you than you are of him," Charley said.

He went back to work. After a while I began to think that Fulgham was taking a long time getting his hand daubed with arnica. Just when I was on the verge of going to the cabin to see what was going on, he returned. He was wearing a glove on his injured hand. Lenore must have forced him to put it on, for Fulgham was one of the tough breed of miners who considered it a sign of weakness to work with gloves.

"You took your time," I said.

"I did for a fact. Dock fifteen minutes' wages out of my pay, Rhodes, if it'll make you feel better."

I was ready to start the ball rolling again, but Fulgham picked up a mud scraper and went out. By evening, when we were together in the cabin, we tried to ignore each other.

Charley was the main safety factor during the hour or two after supper when the wind howled over the ridgelog. The Queen itself was the second saving influence. We had a mountain of hard rock to challenge us, and steel to bite into it, and hammers to strike the steel. When our dynamite had pulled another two or three feet out of Bulmer, there was the shattered rock to be mucked into a tram car that had to be pushed down the track and dumped.

Each morning there was a new face of rock to examine, another round of holes to drill. We ran the tunnel wide enough for two teams to drill the breast, Danny and Fulgham on the left by habit, Davidson and Charley on the right. They were two of the finest drilling teams I ever saw.

Our shift was ten hours a day. Wages were $3.50 a day. I got fifty cents extra as boss, and half of that was to be worthless stock.

Each morning I escaped into the mine as soon as I was out of bed, for every confining influence in the cabin began to work as soon as my eyes were open. Then I returned for breakfast after seeing how the shots had broken. There were few legitimate reasons for anyone going to the cabin, except for meals, once the day's work was started.

The cabin was Lenore's domain. She cooked, learning after a fashion, but she never was very good at it. She kept the place much cleaner than we would have, making the beds daily, sweeping the dirt floor, washing even the coffeepot after every meal. She carried snow in the wash boiler to keep the storage tank full, until one day when she had turned to scoop up a shovelful of snow, the wind took the empty boiler and whisked it away. A prospector came across it three summers later in Warner Basin.

Lenore worked as hard in her way as the rest of us. For a long time I never went to the cabin when she was alone.

Because she was at the Queen I had more time to devote to the mine. Originally I had planned to do the cooking, working it in with the tasks of running the blacksmith shop, framing timbers, keeping the track outside the portal clear, and supervising the work inside.

Now, because of Lenore, I had a little too much time on my hands.

If the Queen ever showed promise of ore, I could go inside and do additional exploratory work, run a raise, or drift off to the side of the tunnel with a crosscut; but the chances of the Creole Queen ever running into ore were remote.

A mine of course holds much more interest for the men who work in it if there is mineral rather than barren rock day after day. But I was satisfied with the Queen. I had tried to tell Delaverne what it was, that the piece of calaverite on the dump of the original prospect hole could have been salted there by Shady Groff, who was not above such acts by any means, as his nickname indicated, or that the calaverite could have been the last bit of residue from ore that had been eroded away a million years ago.

No one was trying to rob Delaverne. We were giving him an honest performance for his money, his stockholders' money, that is. Later on, to be sure we had missed no legitimate bet, I would have crosscuts run on both sides of the tunnel. Some mine owners have a phobia about ignorant employees missing a great bonanza by running just a few feet to one side or another of it. It's like the story of the miner who dug and dug and at last gave up. Another man came along and took one pick stroke and there—riches beyond imagination.

Barren or not, the Queen always met me with pleasant warmth. I liked to listen to the hollow concussions of my footsteps as I went down the tunnel with a waving candle. The rhythmic clinking of hammers on drill heads at the breast said that everything was all right.

I would stand and watch the work for a while and visit during the change of steel, or when one team was shifting from one drilling duty to another. If last night across the table in the cabin Fulgham had been eyeing me covertly, thinking of the best method of hammering the consciousness from me, and I had been holding identical thoughts about him—that was forgotten, or at least sublimated, when we were in the Queen.

If I had glanced at Davidson the night before and then, not realizing it, allowed the glance to become a stare as I turned over personal thoughts about him and his wife, and received from him in turn only a heavy, unreadable look, that too was largely forgotten when we looked at each other in the Queen.

A mine is a man's world. It demands the best there is in him and scorns pettiness. A mine kills him when he becomes contemptuous of it, or afraid, and kills him sometimes when he is neither. The mere act of going underground strips away much of the pretense a man assumes naturally in the open air.

We never argued or quarreled in the Queen, any more than we would have defied the hard, mysterious core of the mountain by whistling when we were underground.

After the first few days at the Creole Queen a kind of dragging reluctance developed in me whenever I thought of doing anything about getting Lenore off the mountain. At first I had been in a frenzy to get her back to town.

Even with snowshoes, there had been no time during the first ten days when it would have been wise to risk a trip down. Then, too, there was a lull when it seemed that we had settled down and could get along well enough, even with the distraction of a woman in our midst. The first, the weather, was a legitimate excuse; the second was a downright lie I tried to make myself believe.

When, after ten days, we had clear, cold weather with only normal wind, I began fashioning snowshoes, planning to make Lenore's first so that she could practice on them while I was making a pair for her husband. There were two torn leather panniers in the shop; they would do for the webbing.

The frames were a problem. They had to be strong enough to guarantee that the user would not become stranded in the soft, smothering snow, halfway down Bulmer because of breakage, and yet they must be light enough to be safely functional. Wood from the native lumber we had was no good—you could not trust it and you could not bend it either.

I finally struck upon the thin fir encasement around a wheel of cheese. It was a straight-grained sheet perhaps a quarter of an inch thick. With no difficulty I steamed it out flat in the shop and cut it into strips about an inch wide.

The strips bent easily into the shape of the bear-paw shoes I had decided on, but one piece of the wood alone was too thin for frames. At least three strips had to be laminated together in some way. I thought of wiring them and knew that was not good. Then Charley suggested glue from the hoofs of the burro.

We got the hoofs at dusk, conspiring with Leonore's husband so that she would not step out of the cabin and see us. Davidson was not enthusiastic about the snowshoe idea. He doubted that I could make a pair fit to hold his wife.

Trimmed and boiled down, the hoofs made a thick glue which, though it smelled to high heaven, held the laminations together. With the leather-punch of my claspknife I drilled holes in the frames and laced in strips from the cowhide panniers. I set two footboards across the frames, with toe sacks on the front crosspieces and thongs on the back ones.

As soon as they were finished Lenore tried them

out on the dump. At first she banged her ankles and stumbled and had trouble turning; nevertheless she rapidly caught the hang of swinging her feet and plopping the shoes down flat.

I went to work on another pair for Davidson.

Lenore found joy in the freedom the snowshoes gave her. The dump was not big enough for her. I came from the shop one afternoon to go into the mine and saw her walking on the bench below. I yelled for her to come back. She shouted and waved, trotting across the snow, showing off. Her feet dipped light from the snow and set it gleaming with a million fairy lamps. She was a tiny figure down there, dark-headed, graceful even on the awkward webs.

I know she must have been happy as she trotted on that great snowfield, teasing me. That is the picture of her that I would like to remember, excluding all others. Lenore against the clean, shining wilderness of peaks, with the cold sun in the southwest, the wind curling away the glitter her footsteps made, and her laughter a shout of youth. I was young too, no matter how I tried to hide the fact. I watched her, smiling.

Davidson came out of the mine, and my smile vanished. He was a stolid, completely uninspiring creature, standing there in his digging clothes. His silence irritated me.

We watched Lenore. When we saw that she was

headed toward the High Place, we both began to yell. She came back then, swinging the webs sturdily, kicking up the sparkling puffs of snow as she climbed toward us.

"Is the weather going to hold?" Davidson asked.

I had the feeling that he would disagree no matter what I said. He didn't want to lose a steady job by leaving.

"Who knows about the weather?" I said. "That's the chance you'll have to take. You can get to Colorow in four hours."

He thought it over for a long time. Lenore came steadily toward us, until I could see the snow-flush on her face.

"All right, make me a pair of snowshoes then," Davidson said.

"I will."

Lenore came to the toe of the dump. She went around the frozen muck and tried to come straight up through a snowdrift instead of angling along the pitch. She put one shoe on top of the other and tripped herself, twisting sidewise as she fell.

I grinned, expecting to see her come up sputtering and laughing, but she lay there oddly twisted, trying to drag her body around.

We went plunging down the dump to her. Her left snowshoe had stuck in the drift when she twisted, breaking the thong, but not soon enough. Her knee was badly wrenched. We got her into the cabin. She sat in a chair, rubbing her knee and trying to smile. She was white-faced. Snow was melting in her hair. When I reached out to brush some of it away, Davidson pushed my hand aside, not savagely but quickly and decisively.

"The best thing is some damp, hot cloths," I said.

Davidson nodded. He waited for me to go outside so that he could expose Lenore's leg. I felt, but I was vaguely angry anyway, even though I had no business looking at any married woman's leg.

I recovered the snowshoes and put them by the shop. Davidson came from the cabin sometime later while I was dressing steel. There was a cracking sound outside the door, but I thought nothing of it for a moment. Then there were more brittle, breaking noises.

When I opened the door Davidson was standing there crushing the snowshoes with his hands.

"What the hell!"

He kept right on, slowly twisting the frames into long white splinters. The act should have been accompanied by terrible anger, clenched teeth, glaring—anything but the deliberate calmness Davidson showed. He finished the job and put the shoes together against the logs, as if he were placing them there intact.

"All right. What's the idea, Frank?"

"She ain't going down."

The way Davidson spoke, I knew his reason was

deeper than the danger of the trip. He must have thought it out in the cabin, because he had no trouble saying it now. "I've decided we'll both stay all winter. At first I wanted her to go back as bad as you did. Everybody wonders what she married me for. They say it won't last long. I'm going to find out about that, Craig. If she's still my wife when we go out of here next spring, then I'll know I'll never lose her to anyone, anywhere."

"That's no kind of a test! Good God, man—"

"I think it is."

"You mean you want to keep her here just to gamble on how sound your marriage is? You mean—"

"Yeah," Davidson said. "To gamble against your brother, you—or the others."

"Me?"

"Yeah, you, Craig."

Even then there seemed to be no stubbornness in Davidson, just a terrible determination.

"I don't get it, Frank." I did, though, and I knew how badly I had underestimated Davidson.

He went into the mine without any further talk. He would have gone to work if Lenore had been lying in the cabin with a broken leg. When he was gone, I tried to figure it out. He was afraid; that was it. He was so afraid of losing Lenore that he was willing to gamble his marriage under the worst possible conditions.

He had been shy around women ever since I

could remember. When he went to church with his mother, the girls used to pester him by staring at him boldly. He would blush then, sitting stiffly in the pew, staring straight ahead at the pulpit.

Then there was a waitress at Sampson's Café. She was a tart and everybody knew it—except Davidson. Miners who fancied themselves as blades used to go to Sampson's in the evening when Frank was there, just to watch his stumbling efforts. The girl led him on for a while, but after she discovered she was not going to get anything from him, not even a tip, she dropped him like a hot potato.

Because he didn't know he had been dropped, he kept going back to the café until the girl took up with a young gambler who was having a run of luck. Danny saw the end of it one night when the gambler came to the café to pick the waitress up. The two of them openly made fun of Davidson while he tried to explain to the girl in his slow, logical way why the man was no good for her.

The gambler got sore and slapped Davidson, which should have been a mistake, because Davidson was as strong as the jaws of a crusher and he was never afraid to fight; but he just stood there that night, still trying to talk sense into the waitress, and the gambler walked out with her.

Danny said it was the kind of thing that made you despise a man and feel sorry for him at the same time.

The test Davidson wished to make now was crazy. Lenore was his wife, and if the union seemed an odd one to most people, the fact remained that she had made the choice without compulsion.

*If she's still my wife . . . next spring . . .*

I went to the cabin to see how Lenore was. She was sitting with her skirts pulled up and bunched around her legs above the knees. The injured knee was puffed. Neither of us was embarrassed.

I took the pan of hot water Davidson had left on the table and reheated it and put it back where she could reach it to dip the cloths she was applying to her knee. Then I began to cook supper, discoursing safely on the merits of sourdough biscuits as compared to any other kind, except buttermilk hot bread.

Perhaps I ran on considerably more than was my custom. At times Lenore regarded me with an odd intensity. If she knew about her husband's intention to keep her here, she didn't mention it. We didn't even talk about her accident with the snowshoes.

When she heard the wind door slam at the tunnel portal, she dried her leg quickly and pulled her dress down. Danny and Fulgham and Charley came in together. Davidson followed his usual habit of going to the side of the cabin to pick up a sack of coal to replace the one burned that day. Until the supply of coal outside was exhausted in the spring, there was always the same number of sacks stacked inside, less the one being currently used.

Davidson put the sack on the stack precisely as he was to lay down every sack he carried in that winter. He dusted his gloves off over the coal box. He lay the gloves across a peg behind the stove. And then he went over to his wife and asked her how she was.

She said she was doing fine.

Davidson tested the water on the table with his finger. I had just reheated it before we heard the wind door bang shut. Davidson glanced briefly at me as he wiped his finger on his shirt. He carried his wife into the storeroom.

"Jesus Christ!" Fulgham grunted. "You'd think none of us had ever seen a woman's leg before."

I was of the same opinion, but because he had said it I told him to keep his mouth closed.

When I opened the log for the day's report, there were other things on my mind besides the Queen. Much later I discovered that Delaverne was almost as fascinated by the human complexities of our high cage as he was by the surprising turn of events within the Creole Queen itself. I stuck strictly to business in the log.

*Nov. 15—Tunnel heading 151 ft. No change in formation.*

# Chapter 7

**O**N THANKSGIVING Lenore cooked one of the two special hams I had sent up with the packer, one for Thanksgiving and one for Christmas. She cooked it too long in a too hot oven, and it was a dried-out lump that tasted like pannier leather. It was enough to make a bitch bite her pups. I walked around on the dump for a while, remembering how luscious and juicy the ham had been before Lenore got through with it.

Charley came out and gave me one of his rare grins. "The gravy was good."

"Fourteen pounds of the best ham money could buy!" I cursed. Charley kept grinning at me, and finally I had to grin myself. "You or I will cook the next one, Charley."

We stood there in the dusk. The thin, lonely sound of a locomotive whistle came to our ears. Then we heard a faint growling from far away."

"Still in Maria Canyon," Charley said.

Ever since the last big snow, engines had been fighting to get through to Colorow. Maria Canyon was a place where slides and drifts always gave the railroad trouble. Sometimes there were three hundred men shoveling down there, with engines slamming their ploughs into the drifts, backing up to scream defiance, and slamming on once more.

From up here on our isolated perch we could

hear the locomotives when the wind was right. An engine whistled again, a pagan sound that was fitted to the wildness of the dusky peaks around us. It stirred some primitive loneliness in me and made me remember the warmth and pleasantness that would be part of the holiday just ten miles away.

"Her knee is getting better," Charley said. "Is there going to be another pair of snowshoes?"

"I don't know." I wanted Charley's help and advice and at the same time I wanted to handle all problems myself. But I finally told him the whole story, everything that Davidson had said.

Suddenly I had a lot of faith in the thought that Charley would know what to do. He lowered his head, looking down at the trampled snow. "The poor devil," he said, and walked away from me.

Sympathy for Davidson wasn't much help. I was disappointed in Charley's response, but I kept turning his words in my mind.

Perhaps it was the heavy way the leathery ham lay upon our bellies that made us so tense and conscious of one another that night as we sat around the table. For the first time since he had introduced it to us, Charley's slide rule held no one's interest. It had been an amazing toy at first and then I had discovered that it was actually a working tool with unlimited possibilities.

Even Danny had been fascinated by it for a time; and Fulgham, surprising as it seemed to me, had a quick mind for mathematics. In fact, he had grasped the principle of the slide rule quicker than any of us. Davidson had caught on too, though more slowly. Every answer that he took from the rule he verified with a pencil. There had been times when all of us made a game of the slide rule, taking turns with it.

Tonight no one seemed interested in anything. I was halfway through one of Delaverne's French novels and had finally come to the juicy part, such as it was. It wasn't much. The French must be more accustomed to sin than Americans, because the reporting of sin in the book was as routine and dull as my entries in the log. *This day I took a mistress for want of something better to do.*

I flipped the book shut impatiently. Fulgham had been playing solitaire across the table from me, but now the cards were disarranged and he was merely sitting, looking at me. He had grown a short, curling black beard since we had been on the mountain. It had not helped the rough look of his face.

We locked stares. Since that day at the High Place, when Fulgham's drunkenness had disgusted me and my fear of height had made me less than a man in his eyes, we had hated each other.

Fulgham and I dueled silently, like two vicious cur dogs meeting for the first time. We would have gone on challenging until something broke, but

Charley said, "Did I tell you boys about the time Joe Mason tried to kill a buffalo with a bow and arrow?"

No one said anything. Charley went into his story. It gave Fulgham and me the chance to look away from each other without losing face. There's no telling how many times Charley averted impending trouble as simply as that. It sounds easy but it could not have been. Charley had to be able to sense the tension when it began to wind too tight, to be a part of it and still above it, and most important, he had to be willing to undergo the emotional strain of being a peacemaker.

I glanced at Davidson. His heavy gaze was on Danny, who was sitting back from the table with his stocking feet resting on a stool. Lenore was sitting at the end of the table toward the stove, reading one of Charley's books. Danny was watching her with a gentle halfsmile. There was seldom anything unreadable in Danny's expressions. Looking at him now was like spying on a man through a window of his home.

Suddenly, in a loud voice, I asked Charley a question about a point in his story. I startled Lenore. She looked up at me quickly and then she glanced around and saw the reason for my rudeness. But Davidson seemed not to have heard an interruption at all, and Danny, that hardheaded young idiot with the drives and fixations of youth, continued to watch Lenore with a musing smile, paying no attention to anyone else.

Fulgham's mouth quirked down at one corner as he looked at me. He pawed the cards on the table and began shoving the deck together quietly, turning his attention to Charley then, as if the buffalo story were holding all his interest. But the insulting smirk stayed on Fulgham's mouth, and I knew he was laughing at me.

I went to get a drink of water, taking the long way around the table. On the way past Danny I hooked the stool from under his feet with my boot. That changed the course of his thinking quickly enough. His feet came down with a thump, and he was ready to fight in an instant. I apologized for my clumsiness without looking at him.

Charley went on with the story. A dishpan heaped with melting snow thumped on the stove. A blast of wind came against the corner of the cabin with a banshee howl and I saw the lights waver slightly in the chimneys of the lamps. There was a singing from the stovepipe above the roof, guyed there with six wires.

Charley told his story with dry humor. I heard only parts of it and I knew that the others in the room were not listening fully either. And yet old Charley and his words made a safety line to which we all clung.

Davidson rose when the story was over. He went to his bunk, and that was the signal to Lenore that it was time for her to go to bed also. Since her accident Davidson had been sleeping in the main room, his bunk rigged up with a tarpaulin bottom in lieu of springs and mattress.

None of the rest of us moved for a time. We watched Lenore as she took a lamp and went into the storeroom. Only Danny said good night. Her reply came back muffled by the partly closed door, "Good night, everyone."

The cabin was growing cold when I woke sometime in the night. Someone had risen. I positioned the sounds a moment later and knew they came from Davidson's bunk. He went across the room almost silently and into the storeroom.

The door shut with its quiet bump.

After a while I sensed that everyone else in the room was awake too. The thick silence of their wakefulness was more telling than any small movements anyone made.

I rose and put coal on the fire. Anyone who wished to say something then had an excuse to do so. Charley murmured, "Feels a little colder than usual, Craig."

Fulgham and Danny said nothing.

I stood by the stove until Davidson came out of the storeroom. A thin bar of light came from the stove, and a window in the south wall let in the reflected glow of starlight on the snow outside. Davidson saw me, but he padded across the room and got into his bunk without speaking.

"For the good of us all, you're going to have to stay out of there entirely, Davidson," I said.

"You can't give me orders like that."

Charley got up and closed the door to the storeroom all the way. I had just as soon he'd left it so that Lenore could hear.

"I'm giving you that order," I told Davidson. "You're not going to wreck everyone's sleep and put us on edge because, by God, you can't control yourself!"

"She's my wife."

"Nobody's denying it. But because we're all jammed in here together, you're giving up one thing."

Davidson was silent for a time. "How are you going to stop me?"

"The next time you go in there at night, I'm going to pull the door wide open, and we'll all be wide awake out here, listening."

"He's right, Frank," Charley said.

You could picture Davidson lying there with his eyes open, staring at nothing, thinking it over. Charley had backed me up. You could feel, too, the silence of Fulgham and Danny across the room, bearing their weight behind me.

"They're young men," Charley said. "They'll be cooped up here a long time yet, Frank. Be fair to them."

Davidson did not answer, but he knew me well enough to know that I was not bluffing; and I'm sure he respected Charley's judgment. I believe the disintegration of the man's slender faith in himself began at that instant when he realized we were all against him.

Charley opened the storeroom door and went back to bed after the silence had held for a time. We all spent a restless night. On rising, I followed my habit of going into the mine to see how much muck we had pulled with the round the evening before. Because it was a blowing day, I guided myself down the wire to the portal.

When I had left the cabin there was a moody silence in it; and things were the same when I returned for breakfast. We avoided one another's eyes. I wished that I had closed the storeroom door before speaking to Davidson.

He was as stolid as ever. You couldn't tell a thing about his thoughts, although the disapproval of all of us was bearing down on him. When we left the cabin as quickly as we could to go to work, Lenore held Davidson behind. I watched him go by the shop a few minutes later.

For just a tick of time I was sorry for him. Before he went inside he stood for a moment at the portal of the Queen, looking down through the gusts of snow toward home.

I was knocking the snow off a log in the timber yard when Fulgham came out with a car of muck. He threw the gate lever and turned the body of the car on the kingpin, but he didn't dump the muck at once. He looked toward the cabin and then glanced at me. There was a safety chain fastened to a heavy tie under the track. Before dumping a car, you hooked the free end of the chain to the frame of the car, in case the muck had frozen and did not spill out loosely.

Not hooking the chain meant taking the chance of putting the car over the dump. Sometimes a man went with it when his clothing caught as the frame upended.

Fulgham did not hook the chain. He lifted the car box with one hand, a feat in itself. The car bucked and some of the muck didn't spill readily, but Fulgham still retained control of the shifting weight with one hand, and emptied the car.

It was a dangerous, show-off stunt, of course, done to impress me. I didn't say anything.

As he came back down the track with the empty car he looked across his shoulder and said, "You're a lousy bastard for letting Lenore hear what you said last night."

That was enough. I had to lick him sooner or later anyway, but as I started toward him Lenore called from the cabin doorway, "Craig, will you come here a minute?"

It was not her interruption alone that stopped Fulgham and me, but, rather, her presence and the excuse we were about to use for fighting. The excuse made us both feel guilty with Lenore watching.

Fulgham put his hands back on the car and pushed it toward the portal. I went over to the cabin. The interior was steamy from a tubful of our dirty working clothes Lenore had started to wash.

"What do you want, Lenore? I'm busy."

"You were getting ready to fight Fulgham."

"You heard what he said?"

"Of course. I heard what you said last night, too, before someone closed the door."

"I meant it."

Lenore nodded. "Yes, I know. I talked to Frank this morning about it."

"What did you tell him?"

"That you were right."

"Fine!" I said. "That settles that problem then."

"Was it so great a problem, Craig?"

"Of course it was! What do you think I'm—we're—made of?"

Her dark eyes watched me with a lively, exploring expression. "Is all your thinking violent, Craig?"

"Since this winter started, yes!"

"Do you hate my husband?"

"No! Why should I?"

"I'm afraid you do. I'm afraid you'll try to hurt him some way because of me."

"No, I won't!" I started toward the door. "Did he tell you he doesn't want you to leave?"

"What do you mean? Of course I'm going to leave as soon as my knee is all right."

"Ask him about that." I went back to the shop. If Fulgham had been in sight, I would have piled into him at the slightest provocation.

Danny came out with the next car of muck. He was carefree in most things, but he was not a careless miner. He used the safety chain on the car. I watched him sourly. When he started back inside, I hailed him into the shop.

"Danny, how far did things go with you and Lenore before she married Davidson?"

Generally he could fend off a question like that with a grin and a smart remark, but now his mouth hardened and he said, "That's none of your damned business."

"I want to know. This whole mess up here is on my shoulders. You've got Davidson looking at you with murder in his heart."

"That's got nothing to do with what happened before. It ain't his business or yours either."

"It's my business to run this mine, and I can't do that if I've got to worry about what happens in the cabin at night."

"The Queen," Danny scoffed. "A hole in nothing! We could all go home tomorrow and save Delaverne money."

"We're still being paid to drive a tunnel!"

Danny shook his head. "Your four bits' worth of authority is making a wild man out of you. Spout off all you want to about the mine, but keep your big fat mouth shut about asking me what happened between me and Lenore."

I hit him a backhanded wallop across the face. He struck me in the chest almost at the same instant and knocked me back against the bellows lever. We wound up outside, hammering each other as we had a hundred times before. We both knew each other's tricks and methods of fighting, so there was nothing to it but pound and hit until we got the venom out of our systems and called it quits.

Danny almost tripped against a rail. While he was off balance I knocked him clear on across the track and into a pile of snow. He came up and punched me in the chest so hard I thought my heart had stopped. There were times when sheets of snow whistled between us so that we could hardly see each other, but we kept on slamming away.

After a while it came to me: there was no pleasure in this fight at all. I was not getting rid of turbulent feelings or my evil temper. All I wanted to do was to beat Danny down as if he were somebody I really hated. I knocked him flat over a pile of logs and barely held myself from going into him with my boots.

That impulse, so narrowly restrained, jarred sense into me. When Danny got up I raised my hands, palms open, and said: "That's enough. We're sore."

"Damn' right," Danny said, and hit me in the jaw as hard as he could.

That was as close as I ever was to going under from a blow by a man's fist. I went down and rolled over. My arms broke weakly at the elbows as I tried to push myself up. Danny landed on me and knocked me over on my back again. Then he began to choke me.

We had never fought like that before. I kept hitting him in the face, but his arms were straight as he bore his weight down on my throat, and my head and shoulders were crushed into the snow so that I couldn't get any real force into my chops against his head. Danny's lips were tight and ugly and his eyes were without reason.

I felt myself going out. I thought, *He means it.*

Suddenly there was no pressure on my throat. Air flooded down into my lungs and I lay there gasping. The wildness was gone from Danny's eyes. "What's the matter with us?" he muttered. "What the hell's wrong with us?"

He got up and went over to the car. I rose and rubbed handfuls of snow on my face. From the way I was breathing I was sure my windpipe was permanently flattened. Danny held on to the car with both hands, staring into it. He said, "I should have stopped when you said to."

"It's all right. You let up—just short of killing me." There was no humor in my words, although I had thought there would be when I started to say them.

We should have been all over our rage, laughing

at each other, each claiming to be the worst hurt. Gubby O'Toole, who had showed us plenty about rough-and-tumble fighting when we were kids, had been proud of us because we always came up from battering each other with no black grudges held. O'Toole claimed that all knuckle fighting should be that way, but Danny and I soon discovered that, except for some of the Irish in Colorow, no one's disposition was sweetened by having the stuffings belabored out of him.

O'Toole would have been troubled by us now. We couldn't laugh. The old spirit of the thing was dead. At last we had got into a fight over something too important to be forgotten quickly. It marked the end of our boyhood together, and it was also the first breaking that would send us down different paths the rest of our lives.

We slunk away from each other. Danny pushed the car inside and I went back to the shop and began to sharpen steel. The knuckles of my right hand ached as my fingers gripped the slender handle of the cathead hammer.

Sure, Danny was still in love with Lenore, and still wanted her. If she hadn't married another man, perhaps he would have forgotten her; but I wasn't sure of that. Beneath his careless exterior there were some deep currents. I was just coming to the understanding of that fact.

And it was of no use to pussyfoot longer around the fact that I wanted Lenore myself.

That night at supper Lenore was wearing overalls and one of her husband's flannel shirts. She had tried to cut the garments down to her size, but it was a poor job of altering. The clothes were shapeless. I decided she had made them that way deliberately. It was an honest gesture, but clothes were not going to change the fact that she was a woman alone with five men.

I sat at the end of the table after supper, looking at my entries in the log. No matter about our personal difficulties, we were doing a good job of breaking ground. We had struck quartz monzonite, a good indication of an ore body in some cases, but it was not the sort of thing you'd care to give a bond on.

At the other end of the table Davidson was reading. I observed that each time he turned a page he was a long time getting his attention set on the following page. Charley had his feet on the oven door. He was silent, smoking his pipe. Fulgham and Lenore were working simple problems with the slide rule. They got along quite well together. If you didn't know Fulgham, you might have taken him for an agreeable man.

I wrote in the log:

*Nov. 27—Heading 187 ft. Broke into quartz monzonite.*

# Chapter 8

WE DRIFTED through the quartz monzonite and ran into solid granite again. There was evidence of a true fissure vein on the contact, so I split the crew and put two men to driving each way along the monzonite where it lay against the granite. It was approved prospecting practice. Up to this time we hadn't even been prospecting; we had merely been spending money.

There was a rough similarity in the over-all structure to the third level of the Royal Tiger, where Fred Bannerman had made his fortune; but so much of Bulmer was monzonite and so many places in the whole district bore resemblance, while barren, to other places that were rich, that I was still unhappy that half my wages were going for stock.

The way Danny had been acting lately it was going to be a chore to tell him that he was a Creole Queen stockholder too. He was no longer my little brother. We were separate individuals now, and I was sensing the division of our ways more acutely each day.

He and Fulgham were no longer boon companions either. Their breaking apart began in the cabin when Lenore began to show interest in Fulgham. Not anything untoward, however. It was just that most of the conversation in the evenings fell to Lenore and Fulgham and Charley. Davidson had always been a rather silent man, and Danny and I were getting that way.

If there was a checker game, it was between Lenore and Fulgham, or one of them and Charley, with the other watching. When there was talk about some of the things Charley tried to get us all to read, Lenore and Fulgham were the ones who did the talking.

Lenore knew what the situation was. She was using Fulgham as a buffer, I told myself. Charley was going along with the game to help keep peace. That was all there was to this business of Lenore's being interested in Fulgham. In fact, I approved of it; it helped take pressure off Danny.

Danny did not share my view. When I split the crew in the Queen, Danny already had it worked out to drill with Charley instead of Fulgham.

All Danny said was, "Let's you and me try working together for a while, Charley."

It was easy and careless, but in the dim candlelight I saw the quick set of Fulgham's eyes when Danny made the suggestion. Fulgham was no fool. He glanced at Davidson and said: "Suits me. How about you, Frank?"

"I came here to work," Davidson said indifferently.

"I'd like to see a little of that out of all of you," I said. "Sometimes I think this hole is getting shorter instead of longer."

We could give and take that kind of joshing when we were in the Queen. The same thing when we were locked together in the cabin would have caused trouble instantly. But I was worried when I went out of the tunnel. The fact that Danny had changed partners was a measure of his interest in Lenore. He was jealous merely because she was being pleasantly friendly with Fulgham.

I went through the wind door into one of the worst storms of the whole winter. The wind was coming out of the south, bellowing, driving snow so hard it stung wherever it struck bare flesh.

If a man had been the victim of what happened that day, the incident would have made a funny story to tell and retell in Colorow. But Lenore was the victim. I guided down the wire and went to the cabin. This time it was for a cup of coffee. That I had to have any excuse at all for going into the cabin during working hours indicates the guilt I held in my mind before I was guilty in fact.

Lenore was not in the cabin.

In this kind of weather there was only one other place she could be, and that was none of my business. I went back to the shop. A half-hour later when I returned to the cabin, Lenore still was not there.

With a violent wind, out of the south for the first time, with the fact that the outhouse was banked heavily on all sides but the north, where the door was, it was not difficult to make a quick guess about what had happened.

I went down the trail to the outhouse and when I was quite close, I saw that I was right indeed. The structure had blown over, door down. I yelled, "Hey! Are you in there?"

Lenore's voice came muffled and furious, "Where the hell do you think I am!"

I began to laugh. She kicked the side of the building and howled, "Get me out of here!"

When I tried to tip the outhouse right side up, I found it too heavy. About halfway up a blast of wind that seemed to have been waiting for such a moment struck like a mighty hand. The building fell forward again and I barely leaped clear. All my effort had accomplished was to wedge the structure more tightly down between the banks of snow beside the trail.

"Are you all right?"

"Get me out of here! I'm freezing!"

I got the whole crew. We considered the problem. Even Charley was grinning. Davidson told us all to go away. He tried the same lift I had tried and didn't get as far. His feet shot out from under him on the packed snow and the building came crunching down, nearly trapping his legs.

Lenore was getting quite a jolting. She asked angrily if we were trying to dynamite her free. Danny suggested that we knock the bottom out of the outhouse and let her escape that way. I said

108

there was no sense in that, or tearing off the roof, either.

Lenore yelled wrathfully that she was fed up with all our talking. You would have thought we were standing in a warm room, instead of in a blizzard, the way she made it sound. We all got hold of the building and made a lift. Even then it was no easy job, and I wondered how Davidson and I, trying alone, had managed to get the thing even part way upright. The wind kept shouldering into us. At a critical point in our efforts Fulgham stepped on a rock under the snow and fell down.

The building wavered but we gave it all we had—and very nearly pushed it over the other way. It was not going to stand alone in the wind, so we held tight and yelled for Lenore to make her escape.

The door was jammed.

Charley ran to the shop for a bar. On the way back he missed the turnoff in the half-light of the storm and plunged belly deep into the snow, dropping the bar. He had to dig it out, and when he came back he was plastered with snow and as near to anger as I ever saw him.

I couldn't keep from laughing, using Charley's bedraggled appearance as an excuse to laugh at everything else that had happened. Davidson gave me a disgusted look. The floor of the building was what was causing the trouble. It had been wrenched until the plank door was so jammed that even with a bar Charley couldn't get it open.

He gave up and began to pry boards off the side of the outhouse, and that was the way Lenore at last made her escape. Without looking at any of us, she stalked to the cabin with more dignity than I thought possible for any human being to have after such an experience.

Stumbling around in the blizzard, we had a devil of a time getting the building back into place and banked with rocks again and braced solidly with poles at the front.

When it was all over, the incident should have been good for some uproarious laughter in the shop, but we went back to work in silence. After a decent interval I ducked across the blast of the storm and went to the cabin. Lenore had washed her skirts that morning, and now they were drying on a wire strung across the corner of the room near the stove. It seemed to me that the cabin was always full of drying socks or overalls or long underwear.

I poured a cup of coffee and watched Lenore from the corners of my eyes. She was still ruffled about the incident outside. "You're working pretty hard around here, Lenore."

"I have to keep busy," she said stiffly.

I kept watching her from the corners of my eyes, and suddenly I saw the breaking of humor around her mouth and an instant later we were both laughing.

"I could just see the bunch of you stomping around out there like clumsy bears!" Lenore's laughter was pleasant to hear. I always loved the sound of it.

"The funniest part was you walking away so feisty, with the wind flapping those sloppy clothes." We laughed again, and it created a fine glow in me to know that we could share humor.

But those few moments of closeness served to emphasize the fact that I had no business in the cabin. Lenore knew why I came. "Did you ask Frank what he told me about you not leaving here?" I said.

"Yes. He said it was too much of a risk to try to get down before there's a heavy crust on the snow."

So Davidson had not told her the truth. How could he? Nor could I. "That means next spring."

"Yes."

"How about that, Lenore?"

"I'll go alone down the mountain if you think I can do it."

She was as afraid as I was of what was growing between us.

"You can't go alone," I said.

Lenore watched me quietly. "Make up your mind, Craig."

"I guess you'd better figure on toughing it out here the rest of the winter. Frank's right about the risk." There were logical arguments to support that view, but my cursed Scotch conscience jeered me for even pretending to logic. "Maybe I should stop coming in here."

"It's your job to make the rules at the Queen," Lenore said. "Don't make any that you can't keep yourself."

"What do you mean by that?"

Lenore didn't answer. She took the cup of coffee I hadn't touched and poured it into the slop bucket near the stove and then went over and felt the garments drying on the wire. I couldn't rightly judge what was in her face when she turned and looked at me from across the room.

But I knew what was in my own mind. I got out of the cabin and lunged back to the shop where there were familiar tools and tasks to help take my thinking from the fact that I wanted another man's wife so badly that I was trembling.

Through the racketing of the wind I heard the banging of the car and the crashing of muck going over the dump. Someone had come out with the car while I was in the cabin, and I hadn't heard it rumbling down the track. It was the wrong time of day, moreover, for anyone to be tramming out muck. That was always done the first thing in the morning.

It was Danny. He stopped on his way back to warm up. I said, "Where are you getting muck at this time of shift?"

"The breast is so loose we can't even drill it. We

picked down." Danny gave me a dark stare. "I thought we were all going to remember she was married, Craig."

"Nobody's forgot it! I went in there to get a cup of coffee. It's none of your business what I do outside."

"Sure. There's no use to yell about it." Danny paused. "We all know she married the wrong man. Even Fulgham knows that. I'm going to take her away from Davidson."

His deadly seriousness jarred me. I hadn't heard him speak with such level determination since he'd said he was going to get the Cormack brothers, one by one, after they had ganged up on him one night outside Poney Adam's place.

"You're not starting anything like that up here," I said. "We've got enough—"

"Oh, I'll be a gentleman about it, Craig, but that's exactly what I'm going to do. When we go down from here next spring I'm going to ask her to marry me."

"She's already married, you idiot."

"To the wrong man."

"You're no judge of that, Danny."

"I think so," Danny said seriously. "There was a time when she would have married me, but I was fool enough to think I didn't want to get married. Now I'll make up for that mistake."

"How do you figure to do that? How do you—"

"I'll be a gentleman, don't worry." Danny gave

me a brief smile but it was not one of his old grins. The devil-may-care edge of it was gone. "You'd better go inside and look at that west drift."

I half expected him to make some excuse to stay outside, but he did not. I followed him into the mine. When I examined the west drift where he and Charley had been picking down, I received the surprise of my life. The monzonite had softened up in the course of one round and the morning pick-down. It was threaded through with talc seams and granite that had been reduced to a crumbling state by some terrific heat action.

We were in a true fissure vein. Wandering down the center of it was a half-inch streak of calaverite, a rich tellurium ore.

Lode mining never carries the excitement of placering, possibly because lode mining is carried on strictly by professionals, whereas a placer miner, seeing a hundredth of the gold that was before us in that thin streak of calaverite, would have bellowed to the mountains that he had a fortune in his hands.

Charley said, "What do you think?"

I shrugged. "It could develop."

We all knew how quickly gold can disappear underground, often never to be picked up again in spite of thousands of feet of exploring; but in the Colorow district a knife-edge streak of pay dirt like the one we had before us was to be followed wherever it led, even if it ran out of the mine and up a tree, for the district was a proved one, and sometimes the merest glimmer of tellurium ore led to immense fortune.

"Who'd 'a' thought it?" Danny murmured. "If Charley and me hadn't busted into it ourselves, I'd swear that you salted the place. Let's take a week off and go down to the Sar and celebrate."

"You're getting docked instead," I said. "We would have found this last week, if there'd been any miners in this hole. There's no use to highgrade either, because from now on I'm having you all strip down just outside the portal every time you come out of here."

"For even suggesting such a thing we ought to break your legs and arms," Danny said.

I went up the other drift where Fulgham and Davidson were working. The formation there was unchanged. Davidson gave me his sober opinion of what he thought was ahead. I went on out to get an ore sack so that we could save the calaverite carefully, and I took some specimens to roast in the oven.

I was feeling pretty good on the way out. If the Creole Queen turned into a producer, Danny and I would stand to profit, but it was too early yet to make any predictions or tell him about the stock. Delaverne wasn't a bad sort, after all; I'd be glad to see him hit it.

After I delivered the ore sack to Danny and Charley, I began to frame posts and caps at the timber station. Under the yellow light of candles I scored the logs with a double-bitted ax down to a blue chalk line, and then used a broadax to cleave the frozen chips away.

I was proud of my ability to use tools, and there was a great deal of satisfaction in the work.

After a time I began to think about Danny and his determination to take Lenore away from her husband. The calaverite specimens were still in my jumper pocket. They would need days of roasting in the meager heat of the range oven before they began to break down. I should take them to the cabin right now.

But that day I did not go to the cabin until everyone came out of the mine.

That night I observed what Danny meant by being a gentleman. He gave up sulking on his bunk after supper and joined Charley and Lenore and Fulgham at the table. They had a checker tournament going. You would have thought the game was Danny's favorite recreation.

Lenore was mildly surprised. Charley was happy to see Danny pleasant and friendly. Fulgham sort of settled down within himself suspiciously. Every evidence of his sensitiveness to varying shades of feeling in people always continued to surprise me. In a situation like that of coming up the trail when we had been lost and freezing, Fulgham had been an animal with an animal's will to survive.

Now he was a thinking man, and remarkably perceptive. He saw the same things I did, so I credited him with well developed shrewdness and gave myself intelligence. I never did quite get over underestimating Luke Fulgham.

Before my very eyes he and my brother carried on their courtship of Lenore. They acted like gentlemen, yes. Danny was charming and Fulgham was pleasant, but underneath both of those qualities was the hard steel of rivalry that grated like a knife on bone.

It was not something you could stop with orders.

For once, Charley missed seeing what was going on. His emotions weren't as deeply buried in the scene as mine. Solemn and silent, Davidson was not misled, I knew. He must have perceived with sharper senses than mine, because Lenore was the only answer he had ever found to something lonely and haunted in the very depths of his soul.

That much I didn't see at the time, for I was no better than the other two young wolves sitting at the table. Let them be gentlemen. I would be something else.

And Davidson, that poor desperate man with an enormous capacity for accepting suffering, did not know how to fight back. The fire of terrible violence had been left out of his makeup, and he was too strong to break and go insane. His only hope lay in Lenore herself.

*Dec. 16—Drifting east and west in vein from station 2 plus 23. Half-inch streak calaverite in east drift 9 ft. from junction.*

That night I heard Davidson get up. The wind was screaming along the mountain, riffling the overhang of the sheet-iron roof, but I heard Davidson the moment his feet touched the floor. He got a drink of water and stood for a full minute silent by the stove.

And then he went quietly toward the storeroom. When I was sure, I said, "No, Frank," and there was a stirring in the bunks across the room where Danny and Fulgham, too, had heard and were listening. All three of us were solidly against the lone man standing in the darkness.

After a time he went back to his bunk and got into it heavily.

# Chapter 9

CHRISTMAS was the coldest day of the whole winter in Colorow. Some thermometers registered forty-five degrees below zero. It was the beginning of a cold spell that ran into the middle of January. Gubby O'Toole was fond of telling afterward that because no graves could be dug in the frozen ground, those who died were put outside for a few moments and then stood upright and driven into the ground with pile drivers. It was one of the few O'Toole stories that I disliked.

On Bulmer Peak on Christmas day it must have been colder than in Colorow. I had put all four of the crew back together in the east drift where the pay streak was holding steadily, widening a little at times, then pinching down to a thin edge, but still leading on into the mountain between well defined walls. The ground was the caving kind; it kept me busy supplying framed timbers, so busy that I had to spend most of Christmas day going back and forth to the timberyard.

It was storming, but the blowing snow created a gloom of its own. And the cold! A deep breath of the air made a pain in your chest, and if the edge of the veering wind caught you with an open mouth, the cold was enough to make your teeth ache.

I hauled lagging from the snow. Most of the poles had to be cut at least twice before they were short enough to handle at the timber station inside. No matter how I tried to cut with the saw, the air currents had a fiendish way of swinging around to jam the blade.

The hairs in my nostrils were like wires and my cheek muscles were stiff and my eyes and nose streamed water. Now and then I went into the shop to warm up, but it didn't help much, for as soon as I went out again, the cold seemed worse. Occasionally turning my back to a particularly vicious blast of wind, I would peer miserably in the direction of home. The layers of snow sometimes whipped aside long enough to see the long swells of snowbanks down on the bench, or even the peaks off to the south.

There is a nostalgia about Christmas that is apart from the true meaning of the day. It was only ten miles to Colorow, but that was a world away. We hadn't heard an engine whistle for weeks. That was the winter no trains got through Maria Canyon for two and a half months. Completely cut away from all our kind, we felt unwanted. Danny had spoken of it in the mine that morning. He said the world had forgotten us.

Out in the furious wind, I hadn't forgotten the world. I knew if I could transplant myself by just ten miles, the magic of friendly faces and friendly greetings would soon loosen my shell of tension and worry. There would be Tom and Jerrys in big silver bowls in all the saloons, turkey dinners in all the restaurants. The mineowners would be tramping around town, getting rid of some of their money to anyone who looked as if he really needed it.

O'Toole would be on his good behavior, having attended Mass for the first time in months, and having spent two months' wages on clothes and presents for kids. He would be in and out of the saloons, booming away with his rich Irish brogue, and he wouldn't get into a rousing fight until long after midnight.

Ma Riley would be cooking a big feed for a houseful of people who were down on their luck. Fred Bannerman would be having open house, and he would invite me and Danny over in the evening for a few drinks, and I would have a minute or two alone with Bonnie . . .

I dragged poles from the snow and went on with my work. Sure as hell Lenore had roasted the ham down like a piece of burnt ore. Again. I had forgotten to tell her how it should be done. I took another load of lagging into the timber station and cut it into six-foot lengths, and then I stumbled back to the shop to warm up.

Lenore came in with coffee in a three-pound lard pail. She put it on the sheet-iron stove.

"Since you haven't been coming to the cabin for coffee, I thought—"

"You know why I haven't been coming in, Lenore."

She looked away from me quickly, setting a tin cup on the anvil. "How old are you, Craig?"

"Twenty-one. You knew that."

"You seem so much older."

"It's the beard," I said. "I'm going to shave after supper, or I'll wind up looking like Fulgham."

"Have you ever been in love?"

"I guess not," I said, and then I thought of Bonnie. I hadn't given a very good answer. "Have you?"

She looked at me directly, but she didn't seem to be answering me alone when she said, "No, I don't think I ever have." She realized that her answer was wrong too. "When do you think there'll be a chance to go down, Craig?"

I shook my head. "Not until spring."

Lenore looked at the floor, and then she went out.

The car rumbled down the track and I heard the banging of metal and the slamming of muck on the dump. Danny came in soon afterward, holding his arms as if they were frozen. "Talk about the ears of a brass monkey. . . . A man could barely freeze to death on a day like this."

He had come out of the even temperature of the mine, warm and sweating, into the bitter cold. We made the change all the time and no one was ever ill.

"Well, coffee!" Danny lifted the bucket on the stove and drank from it. "Now you're being a gentleman."

"What do you mean by that?" He hadn't meant anything, it was only an expression of approval, but I had spoken too quickly and sharply.

"Oh," he said slowly. "I see."

"See what?"

"You had been going in the cabin for it, hadn't you?"

"For Christ's sake, where I get a cup of coffee is none of your business, Danny!"

"Sure, sure. You're really getting touchy, boy." Danny drank his fill and went out.

I yelled after him, "Take that lagging at the timber station on in." I began to sharpen picks. It was Charley's turn to come out with the next load of muck. If they were short of lagging inside, he'd tell me. In the meantime I was going to stay out of the wind for a while.

Work completely absorbed me. Wind rattled the roof, snow clawed at the logs, the bellows squished as I pumped air to the forge fire—and somewhere in the medley of sounds I was aware that the tram car had gone down the track again. Charley did not come into the shop, so after a time I assumed he had gone back inside.

The picks took a half-hour or more. When I went outside to fight the timberyard again, I ran into the car. I laid lagging along the top of the box to take inside. What we really needed was a low timber truck, but—

It struck me that Charley must be sick. I went to the outhouse and then to the cabin. It wasn't Charley who had left the car so long. It was Danny. He and Lenore were standing by the table, laughing, when I entered. She had changed from her shapeless clothes to the skirt and blouse she had worn on the trip up.

They made a handsome couple, even with Danny in his muddy working clothes. Jealousy knifed me. Neither of them was abashed by my appearance, and that angered me.

"Get back to the mine."

Danny's face hardened. "Don't use that tone to me, Craig. You're not Nero."

"Get back to work, I said!"

"Why, damn you, Craig. You—"

Lenore made a protest but I didn't hear it. It was time to knock some obedience into Danny. I took my jacket off.

Charley came in then, his shoulders hunched from the cold. He walked past me and turned around. "I can't blame a man for ducking in to get warm on a day like this." His mild brown eyes held me steadily. He was not the kind of man you brush out of your way, although I could have done so easily. "We ran out of lagging, Craig."

Charley's reason for being there was simple and logical. Yet I think he must have sensed what was going on and would have appeared without a ready excuse.

"Danny was just bringing in some lagging," I said.

Charley shamed us, and the impact of his character held us apart, but of course he did not change us. As Danny went outside, he and I stared a challenge at each other. I began to follow him. Charley touched my arm. "In the last few hours, Craig, that streak is widening like this—" Charley gestured with his hands. "I believe it's going to be a mine."

"Fine," I said. Lenore was watching me. Her change to women's clothes had doubled my desire for her. I wondered what she and Danny had been laughing about.

The car was rumbling into the mine when I went outside. The breach between Danny and me was wide and deep now. Charley said nothing. His shoulders looked thin and frail as he walked away with the wind and snow driving against his back.

Christmas dinner that night was a dismal affair. We were living too close together for any one of us not to feel the change of mood in another. While Fulgham and Davidson did not know what had happened that day, they knew that something had occurred, and their guesses could go in one direction only.

Once I saw Fulgham's gaze jump from me to Danny as if he were wondering if he had two of us to combat. Fulgham and Danny almost knocked heads as they leaped to help Lenore with the dishes. Davidson sat like a lump, his thoughts deep behind his eyes.

I remembered what had happened to two men in Half Moon Basin one winter when a third one went quietly mad and picked up a double-bitted ax one night. I thought Davidson had that look about him. When I asked him a question about the mine, he gathered his thoughts from a long way off and said, "It's looking good." Then, as he stared at the table, I saw him smile, faintly, bitterly.

Charley failed when he tried to get conversation started. He gave up and began to read *Macbeth*. A bunch of Scots murdering each other like sixty: a poor choice of reading material at the moment.

I tied desperately into another of Delaverne's novels. The first twenty-seven pages were about a *concierge* arguing in a market about the price of vegetables with a one-eyed woman from Auvergne.

Davidson said, "I want to talk to you a minute."

We all raised our heads as if we'd heard a gunshot. Davidson was looking at his wife. They went to the storeroom, and before the door closed we heard him say, "It's about wearing those clothes—"

The Davidsons were together behind the door for a long time. Fulgham and Danny kept glancing at me as if they felt I should do something about it. All the while the hellish wind kept ripping at the cabin. Silence and our unspoken thoughts tightened about us like iron bands. The words on the page I was pretending to read were a meaningless scramble.

I banged the dreary French novel together and started toward the storeroom.

Charley said, "A man's got a right to talk to his wife." He watched me mildly for a moment and then went back to Shakespeare.

"Sure," Danny said; but I knew how loudly the silence behind that closed door was speaking to him.

I got the log from my bunk and wrote:

*Dec. 25—Streak in west drift widened to 8" at 36' from jctn.*

Before I realized what I was doing I added:

*Wind still blowing.*

That had nothing to do with the Queen, and the fact that I had let a thought like that intrude into the log worried me. If you couldn't keep your head clear for business, you were slipping.

Davidson came out of the storeroom. We eyed him narrowly. He felt the solid force of our hostility. He looked tired and confused, like one who wished to offer an explanation that would not be accepted. He was the last one to bed. For a long time after the rest of us had retired, he sat staring at the table, until Fulgham growled at him to blow out the light.

Davidson blew out the lamp, and then sat for another hour in the darkness before he went to bed.

Danny and Fulgham went to sleep. I heard Charley snoring lightly, but I knew that Davidson was lying with his eyes open. What went on inside the head of a man like that?

I remembered one Christmas years ago when Ma Riley was keeping Danny and me. O'Toole gave us a steam engine, a beautiful little machine with an upright red boiler, a brass stack, and a nickel-plated flywheel. The alcohol burner made it run like sixty, and there was a little peanut whistle on top that was both a safety valve and a joy.

Davidson came over to see it, wearing new mittens, a coat, and a wool cap his mother had given him for Christmas. It was one time Davidson couldn't hide his thoughts. His eyes gleamed, and I thought he was never going to leave the little engine. When he had to go he stared at his new clothes as if he hated them. He left the mittens behind, and I knew that he did so on purpose. Ma Riley made Danny chase after him and give them to him.

I remember how reluctantly he went away, dragging through the snow toward home. On the way he lost the mittens, and we heard afterward that his mother whaled the daylights out of him.

Ma Riley was about half lit on toddy that day, but she was a shrewd old gal. She suggested that we give the steam engine to Davidson. We were aghast and so was O'Toole, who pointed out the fact that Mrs. Davidson was no pauper by any means. "That ain't the p'int, O'Toole!" Ma Riley said. " 'Tis lack of love the boy has, not wantin' for something to wear or eat."

Charity came naturally to O'Toole, but Ma Riley had understanding.

Naturally, we did not give our steam engine to Frank Davidson. Such deeds make fine Christmas stories, but Danny and I had no interest whatever in the morals of Christmas tales.

To hell with him. He had Lenore, who, by the way, had ruined the ham again.

We all heard Davidson rise in the night. He moved about near his bunk for a while, and then went outside. We had drunk about a tubful of water after the salty ham. I began to doze, but I was aware enough to know that Davidson had not returned. Wide awake then, I wondered how long he had been gone.

The others heard me when I rose. Charley said, "What's the matter?"

"Nothing." I went outside half dressed.

Davidson was in the blacksmith shop, sitting on a dynamite box. I lit a candle and looked at him. He was merely sitting quietly. "What's wrong Frank?" He had put on his boots. There he sat in the bitter cold in his long underwear, pondering.

"What the hell are you doing out here?"

"I couldn't sleep, Craig."

I shivered in the vise-like clamp of the cold. "Stay here another half-hour and you'll sleep for good! Come on, let's get back inside."

He didn't move. I watched him angrily. Fine snow came whistling through a crack and sparkled in the waving candlelight like sunlit dust.

"What's the matter with me, Craig? Why ain't I like everybody else?"

"Come on," I said, "let's go back to the cabin."

"After a while."

The stolidity of him was worse because of his passiveness. Some men you can fight physically and change their actions. There was nothing about Davidson to fight, and his attitude excluded argument. The only thing left was to knock him cold with a drill and carry him inside.

I picked up the drill.

Someone called from outside through the moaning wind.

"In the shop!" I yelled.

Charley came in, his face blue and pinched from the cold. He gave me a sharp look and then put his hand on Davidson's shoulder. "You've scared Lenore half to death, Frank. She was afraid the outhouse blew down again, with you inside this time. So did I, to tell the truth."

"She's worried?" Davidson asked, raising his head.

"She sure is. Let's get out of here before we all freeze."

Davidson went readily enough. Danny and Fulgham and Lenore were up and dressed and ready to come after us when we reached the cabin. "The outhouse blew down again," I said. "Go back to bed." Of course they knew I was lying.

We all settled down again. The wind, the cursed wind, thundered along the mountain.

# Chapter 10

THE COLD that began about Christmas was hard enough to bear, but we were used to extremes of temperature. Compared to the wind, the cold was merely a nuisance. The wind was a potent force that worked upon the nerves. It growled angrily when you closed the tunnel door against it, and it was there waiting to beat you with shrieking glee when you stepped outside again.

Only in the Queen were you safe from the wind, and even then the roaring still sounded in your ears. Even now, looking at the dead pages of the log, I can still hear the wind running on the mountain.

It broke through our thoughts in the cabin. In the middle of a sentence a man would stop speaking, not knowing for a time that he had broken off his words, and he would raise his head and show his helpless fury at the booming of the wind. To be out in the wind was one thing; there you could fight it and curse it and get your work done in spite of it. But sitting and listening to it, or waking in the night and finding it still there, brought on a sense of futility that was close to madness.

Although it was inconvenient, the cold was nothing like the wind. The temperature of the cabin ran in levels. On the floor there was a constant roll of cold air. At the middle of your body the temperature was comfortable. From your shoulders on up, the layer of heat thrown out by the big range was sickening.

Shortly after moving most of our supplies from the storeroom, we had built racks to get the food as far above the floor as possible. In spite of that, disaster struck us. The potatoes froze in the storeroom one night, a few inches from where Lenore was sleeping.

When she showed me what had happened, I made a quick check of our supplies in the main room. A dozen cases of canned food, those on the bottom of the racks, were bulged at the ends. Canned goods in those days were at the best none too safe. Sometimes when you opened a can the contents blew up in your face. When frozen in the can, food was considered poisonous; it often was, too.

Danny said: "Aw, we can eat it anyway. I remember seeing Shady Groff eat tomatoes that had been setting in an opened can three, four days. They never hurt him."

"That's different," I said. "No poison could kill Shady Groff anyway."

Lenore was afraid of the frozen food. She said we could use some of it right away, which we did, but after a few days the contents of the frozen cans had a bad taste. Still later, I discovered that some of the bottom cans in the upper cases had been frozen too.

We didn't throw anything out, right away; before the winter was over it might be better to be poisoned than starved. I began to check the daubing between the logs.

Behind the sacks of coal near the stove, where Davidson had been methodically dumping down a sack of coal every night after work, most of the daubing had fallen out. It had been a rush job to get the cabin sealed; then the bitter cold had helped to crumble the clay mixture, and the daily jarring of a sack of coal against the end logs had really opened the seams.

In examining all the walls carefully I found a good many more leaks where the daubing had crumbled away because of the vibration of the logs in the wind. From the talc-like seams in the mine breast we got material to redaub the cabin. Working out in the weather with a mixture that froze almost as soon as you carried it outside was a miserable job.

I gave it to Fulgham.

From the window of the shop I could watch him and see how long he was outside and how long he was inside the cabin. He had to keep going inside for more daubing every few minutes because he could use only a small amount at one time before it froze. On one trip he stayed in the cabin too long to suit me.

He and Lenore were talking when I got there. They appeared happy. They were obviously not under any of the restraint that affected us when we were all together. It was as if they were free in each other's company, holding some secret from me. Part of my attitude stemmed from lack of experience in authority; the rest was hatred of Luke Fulgham, and jealousy.

The daubing was in a dishpan on the table, steaming from the hot water mixed with it. I walked to the side of the table across from him.

"Something wrong, Rhodes?"

His use of my last name had grown so irritating that it grated against the little patience I had left.

"Get outside and finish your job," I said.

"How long have I been in here?"

"Too long."

"It's a funny thing, Rhodes: Danny stays here half the morning and no word is said."

"He did that once. Get back to work."

"In a minute, when I'm ready," Fulgham said.

Our talk was only a fuse laid to our tempers. We were going to fight and no one was going to stop us. Fulgham steadied the dishpan with one hand and stirred the daubing with a wooden paddle. I could see how set and ready he was.

"Get outside now," I said.

He gave me his down-slanting, insulting smile. And then he gave me the turkey gobble, the ancient Indian challenge to fight.

It was not a too-long reach across the table and I was set for it. With one hand I jammed the dishpan against Fulgham to distract him, and at the same time I leaned across to smash his mouth with my right fist. He was as fast as I was. He stepped back with the dishpan in both hands and I missed him.

Overreached, blocked by the table, I was slow in recovering. Fulgham swung the dishpan at my face. It was full of mud and heavy. I took the stiff edge of it against my arms, but the weight carried through and knocked me back against the bunks. Fulgham came straight over the table at me like a great cat. If my face looked like his did at that moment, the only issue in the fight was survival.

I hit him in the belly while he was still in the air. It was not enough to check him. He came on through, driving his boots off the bench on my side of the table. The impact when he hit me smashed me back against the bunks again, this time so hard that I jackknifed into the opening between an upper and a lower.

Fulgham had me then, but he tried to rush things instead of taking the instant of deliberateness he needed. With my face framed in the narrow space between the bunks, my arms flung wide, I was cold meat. Fulgham hit too fast and hard. I ducked my head and took his blows on top of my thick skull.

He himself hauled me free of the jam when I grabbed his belt as he lunged back. I got in one fair blow that skidded off his jaw and tore his ear.

Where he hit me I don't know, but I do recall that my breath suddenly went short, and that I instantly developed a great respect for Fulgham's power in close. I didn't want to fight him in close, not even if we had had a yardful of room for rough and tumble.

I backed away from him and caught him coming in. His long black hair was hanging down one side of his face. His lips were drawn tight in a flat, animal grin and his eyes held murder. I wanted to kill him.

We ranged back and forth along the side of the table. When Fulgham rushed I gave way and then checked him with long blows. When I had him off balance I drove him back. I split one eyebrow for him. The flesh parted for an instant with the bare bone exposed before the blood came. It was not all one-sided. Somewhere in the first flurry he cracked two or three of my ribs and broke my nose. My advantage was that I was keeping him away and hitting him more often than he hit me.

He cut easily. That pleased me. I intended to make ribbons of his features before I was done.

And then he used my own trick. He let me hit him on top of the head. He came in with a rush that I knew I could not check entirely. I gave with him the whole length of the table and then stepped back at the corner. Fulgham couldn't stop. I nailed him in the side of the neck as he went past. His charge carried him into the woodbox beside the stove. It took him across the knees and he had to throw his hands into the wall.

When he turned he had the tin-can iron in his hand. It was a rod about two feet long with a handle bent in one end. On the other end, built out like the stamp of a branding iron, was a small *O*. The stamp end, after being heated in the stove, was used to unseal the soldered tops of tin cans.

I picked up a Mason jar of sugar from the table. It was only a half-pint jar, but Lenore had filled it after breakfast. Fulgham feinted with the iron. I swung my arm as if to throw the sugar. He ducked, and that gave me a chance to close with him. He caught me two blows on the forearm with the rod part of the tool and one raking blow down the side of the head. I smashed the jar of sugar squarely against his forehead. The twisting shards cut my hand and ripped a long gash diagonally down Fulgham's forehead.

I expected him to go down like a hammered steer. He staggered back with his eyes glazed, but his endless savage strength held him up. Sugar had sprayed out and coated the bloody flesh hanging over one eye.

Fulgham came at me with the iron again.

My hand raked the table for a weapon. I touched a butcher knife and rejected it without thinking. What the brute in me demanded was a club, or something like a club. But there was no handy primitive weapon, and I couldn't take my eyes from Fulgham long enough to find one.

I got his arm when he swung the iron. We bent the rod as we fought for it. We bounced off the water tank and slammed against the sacks of coal. Suddenly I forgot about the unsealing iron. I got both hands on Fulgham's throat. He kept whacking at me with the tool, but the bent handle twisted in his grip and prevented him from getting in a killing smash. He did enough; he left scars on my head that are still there.

I bore him back against the sacks of coal, trying to force his shoulders down. He ground his teeth as he tried to twist free. Saliva and blood ran from his mouth. His face began to darken. I was getting to him now. He dropped the iron, and then all he could do was to try to break my grip on his throat.

I had him. I was going to kill him.

Something kept fluttering against me, making shrill noises, pulling at my arms. I put on more pressure, trying to squeeze limpness into Fulgham's body. He wouldn't go down. I couldn't get him down. I was going to finish him standing.

At last, through the red mist of heat in my brain, I realized that Lenore was beating my arms, screaming in my ear. I looked at her without relaxing my grip on Fulgham. Her face was white and terrified.

Suddenly it was wrong to kill Fulgham.

I let him go. My hands and wrists ached from

the sudden release of tension. I hit Luke Fulgham once more and watched him sag down the sacks of coal to the floor.

I staggered away from him and leaned on the table. After a time the roaring in my head became the sound of the wind once more.

"Take care of him," I said hoarsely. "When he can move around tell him I said to go back to work."

"Back to work?" Lenore stared at me.

"Yes, by God! That's what I said!" I stumbled toward the door.

"What about you, Craig? Your head is—"

"I'm all right!"

I reeled through the wind outside, staggering from one side of the snow trench to the other before I reached the shop. I sat down on a powder box, too weak and hurt to do anything but rest. Fighting Fulgham had been no better than fighting Danny. I felt even worse and was a good deal more used up.

When Charley came out some time later, I was still sitting on the powder box. He looked sick at heart when he came back from the cabin with salve and water in a pan.

I said, "This was one you couldn't have stopped, Charley."

"Do you feel any better about him?"

"I showed him who the boss is."

Charley smeared my cuts with salve and went

back to work. My right hand was aching so bad I wondered if I could ever close it around a hammer handle again, and now I was aware that something was wrong with my chest. My broken swollen nose was a great pain across my face.

In spite of my hurts, when, through the gusts of snow pouring along the mountain, I saw Fulgham come out of the cabin and resume his daubing, I too got up and began to sharpen steel. After a while I went out to where Fulgham was crouching in the snow, putting daubing into the cracks between the logs. He looked as if he had been through a stamp mill.

"How much you got left to do?" I asked.

"I'll finish it this afternoon."

He was not subservient. He was not licked. We were stuck here on the mountain together. There were some things that had to be done for the preservation of all of us. Luke Fulgham was a better man than I had thought. I stayed outside and helped him finish sealing the cabin. We didn't talk.

We hated each other more than ever; but we also were afraid of each other now. With my cracked ribs, breathing in a kneeling position was agony. The blood still oozing from Fulgham's cuts froze in little ridges and beads on his face.

But we kept working until we finished the job.

That night in the cabin Danny and Davidson asked no questions about the fight. Davidson did not even seem interested. He was his usual saturnine self, watching Lenore. He *should* have been silent and solemn. Men were fighting over his wife and he didn't know what to do about it.

I made no entry in the log that night. After letting my hands relax for an hour or so, they were so stiff and sore I couldn't hold a pencil.

That night I heard the bagpipes. The wind had relented a little, coming unevenly in the deep night. Shrill and unmistakable, the sound of pipes came to me. There could not be a human being out on the mountain. I could picture the blue-tinged gloom, the snowfields raising their white dust under the lash of the wind, the wildness of lonely winter everywhere.

Still I kept hearing snatches of bagpipe music, and when I could not hear the notes my mind filled them in. I recognized the tune, "MacLeod's Rowing Pibroch," which old Sandy Reid played often at his home in Colorow.

There was madness in believing what I heard, but it was so. I heard the pipes. And in the morning I had not forgotten. When I went out to go into the mine before breakfast, I walked to the edge of the dump and stood there peering through the blowing snow toward the bench. I saw no track or mark in the unbroken whiteness; but of course the wind would have filled in any marks made last night.

Marks made last night? Did I actually believe I had heard those sounds?

I looked up the mountain then, up there above fourteen thousand feet where the top was lost in ripping snow. By no stretch of imagination could there have been anyone out here last night with bagpipes.

Danny called from the trench that led to the outhouse. "What are you gawking at? You look like a wild billy goat trying to find a place to run."

I went on into the mine, sliding my hand along the wire that marked the way.

# Chapter 11

SOMETIME late in January there came the usual thaw; that is, there was a thaw down in the valley. Some of the roads became visible in broken lines of dark and white, and bare spots grew around the groves of trees that marked farms and ranches. All that was about twenty miles away. On Bulmer Peak, the savage mountain where we had isolated ourselves, there was a lessening of cold in the daytime. The wind still blew, but it was a softer force, playing with the snow instead of hurling it with terrible power.

On the south side of the shop and cabin small icicles grew on the overhang of the iron roofing for the first time. But there was no crusting of the snowfields. That was still months away. Still, it was a pleasant relief to stand on the dump and look out upon the world again, even though you had to slit your eyes to bear the reflection of the sun on all the glaring whiteness.

I had heard the bagpipes several times. The sounds ran uneasily in my head at night, but in the daytime work helped relieve the worry.

I was framing timbers on the dump, reveling in the light and freedom the outside gave, when Lenore came out and stood beside me. She was like a child released from confinement. Her face was happy and the bright glow was in her dark eyes as she looked at the peaks south of us.

I tried to point out the Vesper Tunnel to her. It lay at about thirteen thousand feet, and six miles away, as the crow flies, from where we were, with an unfinished tram that you could see if you knew exactly where to look. She couldn't make it out. I pointed and told her to sight down my arm. I could feel her warm breath drifting across my face as she put her head against my arm to sight.

She said, "I don't see anything but snow."

She looked at me with an apologetic smile. I started to say something, then I just stared. The wind was playing with the hair that lay softly against the cups of her temples. Her face was close, inquiring. A warm expression came in her eyes, and then faded as she watched me for an instant.

That was all I needed. I had been standing away from Lenore for months. Everything inside me went hot and tight. If the wind door of the tunnel had banged open at that instant, I don't think I would have turned toward it. She came into my arms naturally. She was quiet for a moment as I kissed her, until suddenly she began to kick my shins.

Until then I hadn't realized that I had lifted her completely off her feet. I set her down gently, still holding her arms. "I want to talk to you, Lenore, about Frank."

"What's the use of lying like that? You don't

want to talk about Frank and you know it!" Her mouth showed anger and her tone was furious, but there was a soft, lingering look in her eyes that I kept watching. "All you want, Craig—"

I tried to kiss her again. She twisted her head away, kicking at me, struggling. "All right, all right!" I said. I set her down again and stepped away from her, still wild and hot inside. "All I wanted to say is that he's not the man for you."

"And you are?" she asked.

"Yes!" From deep in the tunnel came the rumble of the tram car. I walked toward the shop, and Lenore went with me.

"You've said that before about Frank."

"Yes, and you've admitted it, Lenore."

The sounds of the tram car coming out grew louder. We stepped into the shop and closed the door. A few moments later Charley pushed a load of muck past and went out on the dump and sent the waste rolling down into the snow. He did not stop on his way back to the mine.

Lenore turned toward the door. "That's all you had to say?"

I nodded. She hesitated.

The surging wildness leaped in me once more. I took her in my arms again. Her muscles tightened for another fierce, struggling protest. Then all her energy was diverted in one convulsive moment that turned to a mounting excitement that neither of us wanted to control.

After a moment or two Lenore murmured, "In the cabin."

We walked out and went up the track. Fulgham would be the next man out with the car. The way I felt, I'd kill him or anyone else who disturbed Lenore and me.

I closed the cabin door. Lenore gave a little wordless cry and came against me.

It was Charley who brought the car out again when I was back in the shop. Fulgham had come and gone, and I had been deaf and blind during that time. Now conscience was trying to reassert itself. Through the smoky window of the shop, over the board I had patched into the sash, I watched old Charley on the dump. He had trouble raising the car. He seemed more frail than ever as he pushed the car around the curve and went back to the mine.

It wouldn't do to order Charley not to tram any more. The others in the mine had already offered to take over his share of that chore and he had refused. For me to force him to do less than his share would be wrong, I knew. Charley was proud, but surely he must know that this was going to be his last session of heavy work in a mine.

The way the Queen was developing, Danny and I were going to have plenty of money. Charley Spence's working days were over, come spring.

Danny and I would see that he never lacked for money. Thinking of what we could do for him helped salve my conscience for a while, but it was not long before I was staring morosely out on the snow and thinking of something else.

I told myself that I had to stay away from Lenore, but all the while I knew that it was only beginning.

I went to work furiously, doing all the necessary forge work, and then attacking small, unimportant jobs. I began to wonder if tomorrow would be too soon to go back to the cabin. I wanted to go back then.

At six o'clock it was dark, although the darkness on Bulmer Peak, when there was no storm or blowing snow, was never a real darkness, even at midnight, because everything was white.

On schedule, I heard the muffled *poom!* of dynamite going off in the drill holes. Experience teaches your ears to estimate the kind of breakage dynamite explosions are creating in a mine. The shots sounded hollow to me, as if they were coming from an unusually soft breast, and then there was a queer reverberation that was not normal.

The crew, of course, had hurried away from the breast, not running but moving quickly, after the last fuse had been spitted. They came out when the shots were still sounding, Davidson in the lead.

"What kind of ground do you call that?" I asked.

Davidson thought it over. Danny said: "Drummy, real drummy. Maybe we'll be lucky like they were at the Vesper when they drilled into an underground body of water and washed the whole damned bore out."

"Water behind rock gives back a hard sound," I said, but I wasn't interested in the conversation. I watched the crew go on to the cabin, and then, when I could stall no longer, I followed them.

The evening lay around us with gloomy normalcy. Charley got Danny and Fulgham into competition with the slide rule until suddenly Danny got up and said, "Whoever invented that was crazy." He walked restlessly around the cabin until I growled at him to stay still.

His own tension came snarling back at me, and then he went to his bunk and lay down. Fulgham tossed the slide rule aside and I thought he too was set to pace the room, but Charley began to talk to him about early days in Montana Territory. Charley had been there fifteen years ago, when buffalo were black upon the grass, before Custer disappeared down Medicine Tail Coulee.

But it was not of violence that Charley talked when he spoke of early times in Montana. He talked of the possibilities of growing wheat up there, of Indians he had known, of humorous incidents during the long, desperate winters of the high plains when he had been a buffalo hunter and a wolfer.

Lenore and Fulgham listened to him, asked questions, and seemed contented and interested. Generally the spell of Charley's stories could hold me too. There never was quite enough action in them for Danny. Tonight I caught only parts of what Charley was saying, and there was something in his manner that made me avoid his gaze when he looked directly at me.

Davidson held tightly to his own thoughts, whatever they were. Sometimes I thought there was an odd, waiting expression in his cavernous eyes as he put his slow glance on different people in the room. After a while I sensed how hard Charley was trying. Fulgham and Lenore were not paying a great deal more attention to him than I was.

More than ever I was aware of the hard pulsing of human undercurrents all about me.

I got out the log.

> *Jan. 23—Calaverite streak split into two weak stringers each about 1" wide on footwall and hanging wall at 121' from jctn.*

Those stringers might be pinched out when I went inside in the morning. At any rate, we were making footage, averaging about three feet a day from the time we had started. We had run out of ore sacks soon after striking the calaverite. Ore sacks were something that I hadn't thought we'd have much use for when I was figuring out supplies for the winter.

Piled on ice-crusted flat sheets on the dump, blown over with snow, was the ore we had been saving day by day, about $12,000 worth. Even if the streaks did pinch out now, the Creole Queen was made, at least for promotional purposes. Delaverne had the stock listed on the Colorow exchange at ten cents a share. When he went down with news of what we had taken from the mine, even if no more ore was ever found, Creole Queen stock would boom.

Danny and I would have together about $600 worth at the current price. Overnight it would go up, perhaps ten or fifteen times as much as it was now worth. And still I had not told Danny about our interest in the Queen. Talking to him about anything but the daily work had grown more and more difficult. When we started down I would tell him how I had pledged half his wages for stock without his knowledge.

I kept dreaming over the figures in my mind, but I really was not giving them my full attention. Up here on Bulmer, removed from all places where it had power, money and the thoughts of money could not hold me with full strength. Suddenly I found myself staring at Lenore, remembering the afternoon.

Charley asked me a question. I heard the sound of my name and looked blankly at him until he repeated his words. I answered him. There had been a silence in the room. The wind was not strong, and that added to the odd quietness. Fulgham eyed me narrowly. The jagged scar I had put upon his forehead was still a bright, ugly mark.

Lenore picked up one of Charley's books and lowered her eyes to it. Davidson again gave me his cavernous gaze, and I wondered uneasily what was pacing in his mind.

That night for the first time in weeks Davidson crept out of bed and padded toward the storeroom. I heard him. We all heard him. The others waited for me to order him away from the storeroom. I did not; my own guilt confused me and strangled the order. The door bumped shut softly. I lay in rigid torment all the time Davidson was with his wife.

# Chapter 12

WHEN I went into the mine the next morning, the dull candlelight showed large soft masses of rock blown from the breast in one pile, whereas it would have been normal for the breakage to be strung back from the breast in smaller chunks.

I climbed over the muck pile and stumbled into a treasure room.

Last night's shots had broken into a vug, a cavity in the vein we were following. Almost all vugs are barren, mere pockets in solid formations. This one was not barren. The impact of it was staggering. The walls were lined with calaverite. It had fallen in chunks upon the floor. The breast at the end of the pocket was encrusted with more of the rich ore, and overhead there seemed to be a solid, water-darkened mass of it.

Mining history records only one other vug of comparable richness ever discovered, that in the Cresson mine several years later.

For a while I stumbled around in the small space unable to grasp what I saw before me.

One word, not vitiated then by sloppy usage, describes the vug of the Creole Queen: Fabulous! I scratched the sharp end of the candlestick on the walls. I pried loose chunks of the ore and held them close to the flame to inspect them. It seemed a violation of the careful practice of saving rich ore when I dropped pieces on the floor; but I was already kicking my boots through wealth, standing on it, surrounded by it.

The calaverite was scarcely less beautiful to me as a miner who knew its richness than pure sheets of gold would have been to a tyro. And yet it was months later before I fully appreciated the magnitude of the discovery. The vug became known as Delaverne's Bank. One million dollars was always set as the value of the gold we took from it, but there was not that much gold within my reach, any more than there was a million dollars in the Cresson vug.

In the Creole Queen, within a few thousand one way or another, there was $325,000 worth of gold in the small space, perhaps six by eight, and seven feet high.

The morning I first saw the vug, I estimated its contents at $100,000. I took samples from a dozen places, pounded them all together, and took about one-eighth of the total mass to roast out in Lenore's oven in order to make some kind of guess at the richness of the ore.

After starting outside, I turned and went back for one more look at the treasure room. It was still there. It was not a mocking, unreal thing like the sound of bagpipes on a ghostly mountain in the dead of night.

The air of my own passage blew out the candle

when I trotted toward the portal. I didn't need the light; when you know a small mine well, it's simple to move in it without illumination. I burst through the wind door and trotted toward the cabin.

The sight of the cabin, squat and dark and banked into the snow of the mountain, began to cool my excitement. The Queen was a fresh, living, challenging part of my life, changing day by day, never the same but still offering the same strong, enveloping stability whenever I entered it. The cabin was a trap where we lived too close in idleness, hating each other, feeling the blackness of one another's thoughts.

Everyone else had eaten when I went inside. Faces graven in the same old lines of boredom and dislike looked at me without interest. Inside the mine those same faces had life and vitality and character under the dim light of waving candle flames; but in the cabin they looked at me with a disgusting sameness of expression, with a dislike that was mutual.

Even Charley was getting under my hide. He was too much of a saint. He asked, "How did she look, Craig?"

"It looks fair," I said. "Maybe picking up a little." I sat down to eat, sour because a glorious discovery somehow had faded. The crew went on to work.

After a while I said to Lenore, "We've struck it."

"Oh?" Lenore was not as interested as I thought she ought to be.

I described the vug. I got a little wild and doubled my estimate of the gold in it.

"That's wonderful, Craig. Mr. Delaverne will be happy, and your reputation with Fred Bannerman will be even more solid."

"You think that's all I'm interested in—what old Fred thinks of me?" Lenore's perception of my character was disturbing.

"Why, no," she said, "but—"

"Shall I come in this afternoon, Lenore?"

"No!" she answered quickly, but I saw excitement leap in her eyes.

"All right," I said. But I knew I would be back to see her, and she knew it too. I went outside. The cleanness of the mighty view reproached me. I didn't look upon the mountains long, but went down the track quickly and into the Queen to tell the crew what to do with the ore that would soon be coming out.

I would have it piled separately from all other ore just to see how much actually was in the vug.

The wind stayed with us but otherwise the weather smiled upon us all the time we were stripping the calaverite from Delaverne's Bank. We handled the ore carefully, losing very little of it. I built a platform on the dump, nailing the boards as tightly together as they would go, and sealed the cracks with gunny sacking.

If the Queen had been close to Colorow, with the crew living in the town, high-grading would have been a problem. Sometimes I observed baffled expressions when Danny and Fulgham sadly considered the wealth they were handling, knowing they had no place to hide any part of it they stole. I laughed at them and told them they could have all the calaverite they could carry through the eight feet of snow to Colorow.

We worked without haste in the vug, and it was easy, pleasant work. Within a week all the riches were torn from the walls and piled on the platform on the dump. During that time the nightly tension lessened somewhat. We were able to talk more freely in the cabin.

Once more Danny and Fulgham were working away at their efforts to win Lenore from her husband. They helped her with the dishes in the evening. They joined her eagerly in the simple entertainment of games.

I wondered how long they could hold out as gentlemen. It was quite a strain on them both.

Twice during the week when we were cleaning out the vug I stole an hour with Lenore. There was complete abandon in our meetings, as if we stood on the brink of something that was going to sweep us away. We both realized what a dangerous situation we were creating, but when I entered the cabin and took her in my arms we became drunk with each other. All that counted was the whirling, exploding immediacy of our meetings.

Once the ore was removed from the vug, the long two hours in the cabin after supper again became a time when we receded from one another. Silences became longer, and heavier with unspoken thoughts. A man's smallest action was closely watched by everyone. If one of us went for a drink of water, his movements were followed suspiciously. We examined one another's simplest words for double meaning. We caught each other staring, then looked away, and then looked covertly back again to determine what the other man was thinking.

These of course were all symptoms of cabin fever, and we would have suffered from them in some measure under the best of circumstances. Much deeper and more dangerous than cabin fever was the unending clash of our personalities because four of us were fighting for one woman.

Once after being with Lenore I left the cabin just as Danny was going back into the mine after unloading a car of ore. How much had he guessed? Guilt made me supersensitive to his every mood thereafter.

Gentlemanly as the open courtship both he and Fulgham were carrying on with Lenore might be, it nevertheless brought them to a vicious hatred of each other. Charley perceived it and, in his patient, tireless way, tried to exert a restraining influence on them.

Lenore was the focal point of all the swollen thoughts that lay unspoken in the cabin during the charged hours of the evening. Though she must have been under a greater burden than the rest of us, she hid her feelings and did all she could to help Charley in his struggle to hold us to decent behavior. She followed every lead he opened to divert our minds from silence and brooding.

She continued to wear men's clothing. After the first shock of seeing her dressed so outlandishly, we had grown used to the garments. They made her look odd but they could not change her. Her hands were beautifully expressive, and her voice stirred our imaginations and made us remember every desirable woman we had ever known, including some we should not have remembered.

Her dark eyes, meeting mine suddenly, made me forget that there were others in the room. I saw the same forgetfulness come upon Danny and Fulgham too. They watched the turn of Lenore's head, the lamplight gleaming on her blue-black hair, the delicacy of her wonderfully alive features. She created a torment in all of us. It was not her fault, of course; but some of us had more reason to feel tormented than others.

Davidson was sinking deeper and deeper into his own thoughts. Sometimes he sat for an entire evening with his powerful shoulders bent, staring at a book without ever turning a page. The tight cap of his hair, bowed toward the lamp, looked like frowsy orange wool. At times I would allow myself to forget that he was Lenore's husband, or to underestimate him as a man. Then, suddenly, I would sense the impact of his gaze, and turn to meet his disturbing, unfathomable eyes.

The longest part of the winter was still ahead, the wearing, grinding months of February, March, and April.

Some of the worst storms of the winter would come during the next three months. Down in the valley the snow would melt quickly and men would be talking hopefully of spring, but here on Bulmer Peak shaded hollows would hold deep drifts of snow until August. Unless we had miraculous weather, mid-May would be the earliest we could hope to start down.

Even if there had been no woman with us, I still would have had enough to worry about. For one thing, spoilage had cost us eight cases of canned goods. Some of the rest was doubtful. Our sacks of potatoes had turned black and we had thrown them over the dump. Weeks ago I had told Lenore to make our supplies stretch as far as possible; but, though she tried, she wasn't a very good manager.

The Creole Queen itself, however, was a factor that helped to ease the food situation. Ever since we hit the soft, tight formation that led to the vug, we had been breathing bad air. That helped to rob the appetites of those who worked inside for most of the shift; it also made them more irritable.

The run of good weather changed early in February. Once more the monstrous wind came bellowing. We shoveled snow to make our limited movements on the dump, digging it away from the tunnel door every morning, and pitching it down into the deep channel just outside the portal. We held to the guide wire as we stumbled along with the snow rattling against our backs when we went to the mine. Twice daily we picked glittering ice from the ditch for twenty feet inside the tunnel.

One day when Danny was picking ice from the ditch and I was framing posts at the timber station, I stopped working and went over to him with the broadax in my hands.

"We've made a mine," I said.

"Yeah."

"I want to tip Fred Bannerman off before the news gets around." Old Fred had plenty of money, but I never knew a rich man who would turn up his nose at making more.

"Sure," Danny said. "That won't hurt."

"I also want to borrow $1,000 from him for you and me to buy stock before it goes wild."

"That'll be good, if you can do it."

"He'll do it, if you don't try to bargain with him in advance. If you tell him the truth and then ask him for the money—"

Danny scowled. "What are you getting at, Craig? What do you mean, '*Me tell him the truth*'?"

"The Queen is fairly well made. You and Fulgham can rig up snowshoes and go down if you want to. It won't be easy, and I'm not trying to force you to—"

"Let's all go down."

I shook my head. "I don't think Lenore and Charley could make it, and Davidson won't even try."

"Why won't he?"

"He won't!" I said angrily. "Just take my word for it."

"All right. Then let's you and me and Fulgham try to get out. We can bring back snowshoes and a toboggan for Charley and Lenore."

"And then all of us go down?" I asked.

"Sure. You said the Queen was made."

"I still don't want to shut it down entirely. I'm being paid to work here all winter."

"Delaverne won't give a damn, after he finds out what we've hit."

"That's not the point." I fingered the long blade of the broadax. "You and Fulgham don't want to go out, huh?"

"*I* don't." Danny gave me a searching look. "Ask Fulgham yourself what he thinks."

"All right; we'll stay." I shrugged but I was furious as I turned to go back to the timber station.

"I'm playing it fair with Lenore," Danny said. "The way you beat around the bush trying to get rid of me and Fulgham don't sound right." He walked up close to me. "You're playing it fair, aren't you?"

"Don't be a damn' fool, Danny." I started away.

"I asked you. Are you?"

I told my brother the biggest outright lie that ever stood between us. I looked him in the face in the dim tunnel light and said, "Of course I am. Did you and I ever lie to each other about anything important?"

Danny watched my face in the gloom. He nodded. "No, we never did." Satisfied, he went back to work.

On my second or third stroke with the broadax I sent the clean, beautiful edge of the tool into the iron dog that held the log to the bedding timbers. It was the clumsiest stroke I had ever made.

A half-hour later, when Danny had finished cleaning ice from the ditch, he went on up the tunnel toward the breast, and I stood feeling the blunted edge of the ax, reviling myself for lying to him.

All settlements seemed to be delayed until some time in the future when we would be away from the Creole Queen.

That afternoon I went once more to Lenore. I wanted her. That much was always clear. After every meeting I told myself that what I was doing was wrong, but when we were together there was no right or wrong.

That we would be found out sometime was inevitable.

The wind was howling overhead one afternoon as we lay together, at peace for the moment. Footsteps crunched in the ice and snow outside. The door latch raised and the door scraped back on the sill. I leaped up.

Charley stood framed against the storm, with snow on his stained Scotch cap, his face grim and hollow-cheeked. He was there only a moment. He turned away and pushed the door shut.

I found him later in the shop, standing close to the sheet-iron stove with his hands spread to the heat. He was the only man I ever knew that I feared, and yet there were only love and compassion in him. I knew that if he had wished to do so, he could have scourged me with words of fire.

He said, "Do you think you love her, Craig?"

I didn't know. In honesty I could not have said that I loved Bonnie either; she was too confused with my ambition.

"I don't know, Charley."

"There is another man that does."

That was all the rebuke that Charley gave me, but it was as powerful as the Sermon on the Mount. He warmed himself and started back to work. I noticed how much trouble he had with the wind against the door. I sprang to help him.

That night, staring at the log, I felt Davidson's eyes on me. When I met his look I was almost sure that he, too, knew about Lenore and me.

For some time he had kept a candlestick stuck in the wall at the head of his bunk, the sharp end driven deeply into the log, as if he had sunk it there while angry. The strong hook on the side, needlepointed, was curved toward the inside of the room.

I considered taking the candlestick back to the portal where it belonged with the other spare ones; and then I told myself that it would be admitting that I feared Davidson if I moved the candlestick. Besides, I knew that it would appear again in the wall by his bunk if I took it away.

Perhaps the damned thing meant nothing; a guilty man always sees figures moving in the shadows of his own mind. I remembered the story O'Toole had told me of the young tailor in Mexico City who was carrying on an affair with his employer's wife. In the daytime, sitting cross-legged on the counter as he worked, the young tailor would watch his boss walk past him slowly with a long pair of shears. The employer never glanced at the other man; he merely drifted past him a dozen times a day, slowly opening and closing the sharp clothing shears. After a week or so the guilty man left the country. According to

O'Toole, the husband had never even suspected the young tailor.

I kept glancing at Davidson's candlestick.

I made my entry in the log:

*Feb. 6—Calaverite 6" on hanging wall*
*17' from east end of vug.*

Twice during February the weather got into the log: *Wind still blowing* and *The wind is never still.* Once I wrote something about the sound of bagpipes, but I marked that reference out carefully as soon as I realized what I had done.

# Chapter 13

ONE MORNING before breakfast I started as usual to the mine to make my early inspection. Reference points only a few feet away were blanked out by a howling storm. I was guiding down the wire. For a distance beyond the shop there was an area relatively free of snow, where the deep trench ended. When you were in the trench itself, you could not go wrong, but I always used the wire anyway, from force of habit.

Suddenly I found myself crowding against one side of the trench, but before long I was out of it and into the cleared area where the snow was only about six inches deep. I could feel it streaming against my legs as I walked. I almost turned my ankle when I stepped on one of the track rails with my left foot. The wire should have kept me in the middle of the track. I laid my wandering to the fact that I was lurching along blindly, probably pulling slack in the wire toward me. I moved a fraction to the right, guiding on the wire, trusting it as automatically as an old woman puts faith in a banister while going downstairs.

Something, possibly the unevenness of the going underfoot, made me stop and stand uneasily. Where we walked between the rails the snow was hard packed. Where I stood the snow felt loose. I began to kick about with my feet to find the rails. I could not find them. I must have gone too far to the left. How could I, guiding on the safety wire?

Suddenly I was as lost as the day I had missed the shop and wandered in panic. The channel somewhere ahead worried me. We had thrown snow from the daily drifts against the portal into it, and ice from the tunnel ditch, but the channel was a mighty windway scoured down to the rock in places. A plunge into it could cripple or kill a man.

I went on a few more steps and stopped. I could have gone back, of course; but to return was like admitting that there really was a bagpiper on the mountain, and that I was losing my grasp on reality.

No, I would not turn tail; I knew that the wire led to the portal. I was confused, that was all; just as I had been confused before in blinding storms on the mountain.

I went on another few steps and stopped again. Something was terribly wrong. Still, habit was so strong that I had to force myself to let go of the guide wire and cast about. I blundered off to the right without finding the rails. Almost in panic, as I went back to the left, my foot struck steel. I knelt and grabbed the rail beneath the moving snow. There had to be another one only eighteen inches away. Raking the snow with my free hand, I found the second rail. There could be no treachery in the track; it had to lead directly to the portal.

Kicking all the way against the rails, I stayed with them and went on to the portal, stumbling into the drift against the wind door before I was sure where I was.

The guide wire was not around the spike where it belonged on the right side of the portal. I kept groping until I found the wire, four or five feet off to the right, turned around a moil driven into a crack in the granite.

If I had kept to the wire I would have walked off into the channel, plunging fifteen feet onto the rocks and ice. I replaced the wire where it belonged and went back to the cabin.

Danny was frying sidemeat, Fulgham was watching the coffee, and Charley was setting the table for Lenore.

A fine, helpful group, I thought savagely.

Davidson was doing nothing; he never could seem to find a chore inside the cabin.

"Who moved the wire?"

No one answered. They looked at me with vacant expressions, or sullenly. All but Charley. I saw the quick lift of intelligence in his eyes, and knew that he had grasped the situation instantly.

"Who moved the wire!"

Charley said, "Are you sure it *was* moved, Craig?"

"A few more steps and I would have fallen into the channel!"

Fulgham said, "That would have been too bad."

I started toward him, but Charley came between us instantly. "You can't settle anything that way, boy."

"God damn all of you! Who moved that wire?"

No one answered. Danny was angered by the accusation and Fulgham was belligerent, but Davidson sat with an empty expression, as if he had not grasped all the facts yet.

I looked hard at them all. "Who was the last man out of the mine last night?"

"I was," Charley said. "I brought the car to the timber station and loaded it with lagging while the others went on out."

"Somebody moved that wire!" I was shaking with rage.

"Fulgham?" I asked.

He looked at me contemptuously, without replying.

"Davidson?"

He stared at me blankly, almost stupidly.

After a short silence Fulgham said, "Why don't you ask Danny, or is he too pure for you to suspect him?"

"God damn you, Fulgham!" Danny said, and started forward.

I grabbed the pick handle at my bunk, but it was Charley once more who stopped trouble before it began. He stood bent and quiet before Danny's rage, and turned him back without a word.

"I was the last one out," Charley said. "I don't

remember paying any attention to the wire because it wasn't blowing enough to need it at the time."

"Who went out just before you?" I demanded.

"Everybody."

If Charley had a good idea of who had changed the wire, he wasn't going to say. It was either Davidson or Fulgham, of course. I looked at the candlestick in the wall by Davidson's bunk, then I looked at Fulgham, hating him as he hated me.

"I'll have the truth." I lifted the pick handle. "Fulgham, I'll start with you."

Fulgham had been waiting for my move. He slid along the table, knocking Davidson out of the way, leaped to the stove and grabbed the double jack we used to break large chunks of coal. "Come ahead, Rhodes."

I edged toward him. I would draw him into making a hard swing with the hammer. Missing, he would be badly off balance, and then I would have him.

"What kind of barbarian are you, Craig?" Charley's voice was quiet. They were the same words he had used before to shame Danny and me when we went wild. If he had shouted, I wouldn't have heard him, or if it had been any other man speaking I wouldn't have listened.

I hesitated, realizing that I was moving, not so much from a desire to pound truth from Fulgham, but because I wanted to crumple him to the floor with slashing strokes of the pick handle, to beat him down because I hated everything about him.

He stood with a wolf grin streaked across his black beard. The scar I had made on his forehead was bright against his pale skin.

"Come ahead, Rhodes," he said, and I forgot about Charley.

Fulgham knew as much about the distribution of weight in a hammer as I did. He made no wild swings when I tried to feint him into doing so. He pawed with the hammer instead, keeping one hand close to the head of it, gripping the long handle at the very end with the other hand. It was never out of control and he poised it high enough to protect his head.

He almost caught me in the face with a chopping blow. He laughed when I leaped away. I used the pick handle like a foil then. I jabbed him in the face with it. Feinting an overhead swing, I stabbed the square-cut end into his face again.

Fulgham lost his temper and swung the hammer hard, with both hands close to the end of the handle. He couldn't recover quickly enough. I dazed him with a blow that left a welt across one ear and the side of his head. He was set up for the kill.

Danny stopped me by crashing into me with his shoulder and driving me back along the table. As we struggled for the pick handle, Danny shouted: "You heard what Charley said! Are you crazy?"

Charley took the hammer from Fulgham, who gave it up without protest.

"All right!" I growled at Danny. "Get your hands off me." I tossed the pick handle on my bunk.

"Remember how you used to curse when you heard stories about pick-handle bosses?" Danny asked. "What's the matter with you, kid?"

"Somebody tried to kill me." I stared at Fulgham, but he looked back at me steadily, without fear. I looked at Davidson. His expression was still bewildered. Lenore's head was bowed, and she wouldn't look at me. I knew she hadn't moved the wire, and neither had Charley.

Danny said, "You'd better forget it, Craig."

Forget it! Suddenly my distrust reached out to include my own brother. I turned from him and said, "It's time to go to work."

"Everybody generally eats breakfast first," Charlie said mildly.

I went outside and stood in the lee of the wind at the front of the cabin. Fulgham too was too full of poison to eat, and he came out ready for work. We stared at each other, and I thought he was going to say something, but he turned away into the white hell of the wind.

When the others came out to go to work, I held Charley back and asked him, "Did you tell Davidson about me and Lenore?"

He gave me a look of reproach. "No, but he knows. He's no fool." Charley turned up his coat collar. One moment he was beside me, and then he took a few steps and disappeared into the storm.

I went back into the cabin and began to rummage through the bunks. Laid in a little niche where the chinking ran out beyond the curve of the logs by Fulgham's bunk I found a starter, a short drill. There was one in Danny's bunk too. Davidson, of course, still had the needle-pointed candlestick close to his pillow.

"How long have they been taking these things to bed with them?"

"I don't know," Lenore said.

"You make the beds. You do know!"

After a moment she said, "Since about the time Frank put that candlestick in the wall."

It was shocking to know that we had drifted so far into distrust that we were going to bed with weapons close by. I was in it too; I had been keeping the pick handle within close reach every night.

"You mustn't come in here any more in the daytime," Lenore said softly.

I nodded. "You're right." As we looked at each other, I knew that we both doubted that we could hold to the resolution.

The wind died suddenly that afternoon. Clouds the color of an old bullet came up in great masses to the west. It was snowing when we ended the shift, a quiet snow that fell almost straight down. Inside the cabin the quietness was oppressive. It was as if the weather had prepared a strange, silent background for some change in our lives.

Lenore went to bed in the storeroom as soon as the dishes were put away. Charley got into his bunk a few minutes later, slowly, as if he were dead tired. The rest of us sat at the table in silence for a while. When I wrote in the log everyone watched me intently.

Sometime during the night the wind returned with enough strength to fret along the cabin walls and moan faintly at the corners.

Again I heard the bagpipe music as if it were within the room itself. I knew it was not there. I knew, too, that long ago we should have taken a wild chance and tried to get off the mountain; for now, at least in my case, I was slipping from the world of reality.

Someone rose. I thought it was Davidson at first, and then I knew it was someone across the room. I heard him dressing. The door grated, and I saw Danny's figure outlined against the snowlight.

He crunched around outside. Once he bumped against the cabin logs. I rose and began to dress. The sound of the pipes came to me as I was putting on my mackinaw, and then I heard Danny laughing to himself outside. He's gone crazy, I thought.

The snow had stopped. Starlight was striking fire from the white fields. A feeling of tremendous height and coldness came from the mountains.

I found Danny chest deep in snow at one corner of the cabin, staring at something above his head. I saw his grin when he looked at me.

175

"There's the damned violin," he said, and pointed upward. "I don't mind saying that it bothered me some, Craig."

"Sure, sure, Danny. Let's go back inside now." I felt sick.

"There, you see!"

Then I heard the bagpipes again.

There were six guy wires on the stovepipe. When the wind struck them with a particular force, they played thin music that ran down their quivering lengths into the snow on the roof. Danny had thought it was a violin, while I had heard a bagpipe.

We stood there laughing, weak with relief. Charley called from the cabin door, "What's the matter?"

We went back inside and told him. "I thought I was going nuts," Danny said.

"Why, sure, the guy wires," Charley said. "I've been hearing them for weeks, but I knew what it was all the time."

We went back to bed.

Though Fulgham and Davidson were awake, they made no comment. They had heard the guy wires too, but what had they thought the sound was? That none of us had talked to another about the music seemed darkly significant.

The night was not done yet.

Once more someone woke me up. This time it was Davidson. He dressed, put on his boots, and went outside. When he didn't return I remembered the night I had found him sitting in the shop, freezing. Damn the man anyway; let him freeze! But I rose and dressed a second time.

Lenore was up by then.

"*Now* what the hell?" Fulgham grumbled.

"Never mind," I said. "Stay in bed."

Lenore and Charley and I went out to look for Davidson. He was not in the shop or on the dump or anywhere else in sight. He must have gone into the mine.

I stood by the shop, shivering and angry and disgusted. "What's the matter with him anyway?"

"You know," Charley said. "He's punishing himself."

"For what?"

"For moving the wire. For trying to kill you."

"Then you did know!"

"No," Charley said. "I didn't see him do it. Lenore knows it as well as I do."

"Yes," Lenore said. "I do. But we've got to find him."

"He's crazy!" I said.

We started toward the mine. On the near side of the place where the track crossed the channel I saw Davidson's trail. He had gone straight up the mountain, starting where the snow was chest deep. We followed, wallowing and falling and gasping as the snow cascaded down on us from the edges of the trench Davidson had made.

We found him about a hundred feet away, sitting where the wind had scoured the snow down to dark rock. He did not move as he sat there watching us claw our way up to him. I wanted to curse him, to kick him back down the hill. I shouted to him angrily.

He raised his head. In the snowlight I saw the tortured expression on his face. He said brokenly, "I'm sorry about the wire, Craig."

The anguish in his voice cut the ground from under me and left me helpless and ashamed. I stood there on the quiet mountain, panting from the climb. Davidson watched my face, but when I said nothing more he lowered his head dumbly.

Charley and Lenore came struggling up to us. I could feel the coldness in my chest.

Lenore knelt on the icy stones beside her husband. "Shall we go back to the cabin, Frank?"

Davidson nodded, without saying a word.

Lenore put her arms around him as one would comfort a sick child. I wondered how she felt. Charley touched my arm, nodding for me to go back. I walked down to the track. Miserable, and shivering in the cold, I knocked snow from my clothes and stared down in the direction of Colorow.

Up on the mountain Lenore and Charley were talking quietly to Davidson, and then it was just Charley who was speaking. Presently I saw them all coming toward me.

# Chapter 14

CHARLEY SPENCE was dying all the time he was with us at the Queen.

Some men gather years and nothing more as they run out their brief span on earth. But Charley had come to peace with himself somewhere along the line. He must have been a hell-binder once. I suspected it because of the things he did not tell rather than the things he did say.

He understood all of us better than we knew ourselves. We were young, although we had been acting like men and doing the work of men for six or seven years; but none of us was mature. Under the circumstances, that Charley was able to restrain us from complete savagery and selfishness was little short of wonderful. But he gave himself to the task because he was a man full of love. I think God had breathed upon him and touched his spirit.

For a short time after Davidson went out on the mountain to freeze, our guilt sobered us into better relations with one another. We made no objections to his going to the storeroom at night. The physical part of his being with his wife was not, I am sure now, the important factor in Davidson's mind. He was afraid of losing her to one of us. Perhaps he already thought he had lost her to me. He wanted some kind of assurance that this was not true, and he went to Lenore because she was his only source of strength and confidence.

We didn't let Davidson and his wife maintain normal relations for very long. It was too much for us to lie awake in the big room and let our imaginations work. We blocked Davidson away from his wife once more. This time Danny and Fulgham did not leave it all to me. They too roused in their bunks and snarled at Davidson when he rose in the night. Though we beat him down with something worse than violence, and stripped from him what little confidence he had in himself, the union of Danny and Fulgham and me against one individual gave us a certain sense of solidarity, despicable as it was. It helped us to tolerate one another.

Dragging time brought the month of March at last. A wet snowstorm came slanting from the east before a more temperate wind. The storm began in midmorning. I walked back and forth from the end of the trench to the narrow crossing above the channel. I exulted. Warmth would settle the snow-fields, and consolidate the top crystals of the snow into a strong crust. This wet storm might be the harbinger of an early spring that would extend its warmth even into the timber. On some bright moonlight night we could walk away from the mountain on a solid surface.

The wind changed before noon, resuming its usual direction from the west. The warmth went from it, and the snow came down hard and bright, no longer sticky. I went down from the dump and tested the snow. When it froze there might be a crust an inch or two thick under the new fall. That was all.

I fought my way back to the dump, cursing the elements which had thwarted me. Through the falling snow the big cabin loomed darkly against the mountain. It was a cage for all of us.

I looked sourly at the piles of ore upon the dump, and at the timberyard, where the logs were going fast. Suppose some well intentioned idiot came tramping up here on snowshoes one day to see how we were. He would find out about the strike and go rushing back and ruin my chances to let a few friends buy stock before the market soared. I cursed and went toward the mine. Since the day Davidson had changed the wire, I had never trusted it again. I guided on the rails instead. Above the channel I paused to look down. The wind was steadily bearing the snow away. I saw the tops of granite rocks.

The clink of hammers against steel came to me as I walked toward the tunnel breast. It was a familiar sound, and I welcomed it.

Hand drilling, an art long lost, was beautiful to watch. Working side by side, both teams had almost finished cut holes, down-slanting holes

181

that, when loaded with dynamite and fired, would wedge out the center section of the breast.

On the left Fulgham and Davidson were drilling, Fulgham holding and Davidson striking. On the right Danny was holding, or turning the drill, while Charley was striking. It was a narrow tunnel; there was just room for the two teams to work together.

The hammers flashed back and forth precisely, powerfully, steel coming down to meet steel. The area of contact on the drill heads was no larger than a dime. Any variation of a straight, true drive of the hammer beyond that limited area was a waste of power. Charley was what we called a "tapper-light," a striker without the power of men like Davidson, but one who hit eight or ten strokes more per minute. Charley's striking matched any man's performance.

Davidson was stolid and slow. His hammer blows were steady, meeting the drill with terrific force. On rare occasions when his swing was off a trifle and came in against the drill even minutely out of true line with the steel, the shock was enough to send a sharp tingling up the arm of the man holding the drill.

I watched, pleased by the precision and power of the craftsmanship before me. Danny was sitting on a muddy powder box, holding and turning with one hand. Each hammer stroke that Davidson made flashed past his head about a foot away.

After a while I couldn't take my eyes from Davidson's hammer, and as I watched him fear grew great inside me. I tried to believe that it was out of proportion to the facts, but I couldn't convince myself. Davidson's hammer continued to sweep close to the back of Danny's head. My brother caught something in my expression. Still turning steel with one hand, he gave me a curious look, and the moving of his head put it inches closer to the flashing hammer.

If I was thinking desperate thoughts, why wouldn't like ideas lie in Davidson's mind? Even if he wasn't crazy, he had been brooding for so long now that I felt I could no longer trust him. I was terrified by the sight of that hammer passing so close to Danny's head.

Charley was striking too, much faster than Davidson. The steady movements of the hammers threw monstrous shadows on the walls.

"Hold it, boys!" My voice was hoarse and tight. The drilling stopped. The four men turned their heads to look at me.

I motioned toward the west drift. "I want to do some exploring in the other drift. Davidson, you and Fulgham gather up your tools and come with me."

Later, in the shop, Charley asked me, "Why'd you make the change?"

"Because I'm afraid to have Danny and Davidson close together."

Charley nodded. "That's what I thought."

"What are we all afraid of, Charley? We've got drills and candlesticks stashed around our bunks. I've got a pick handle. What's the matter with us?"

"You know as well as I do."

"You don't have a drill in your bunk. Aren't you afraid that some night Davidson will go crazy—"

"He could run wild, yes," Charley said. "I've seen quiet men like him do that, but I'm not afraid—not for myself, that is."

"You haven't done anything to Davidson."

"No, I haven't, except that I failed to protect him from the rest of you."

"No one could have done that," I said. "It was up to him to fight for his wife. All he does is sit around and make us afraid of him."

Charley watched me quietly. "Or are you afraid of yourselves, Craig?"

"He's as much to blame for what happened between me and Lenore as we are!"

"Is he?"

"Anyway, that's all over."

"I'm glad to hear that," Charley said.

"Who will he go for if he does go nuts?"

"You."

Charley went back to work.

Two weeks after I put Davidson and Fulgham to work in the west drift they opened up ore. Eventually we would have found it anyway, for the whole area was thoroughly explored before the Queen's short span as a big producer ran out; but there seemed to be mockery in the fact that every move I made inside the mine was marked with success, after I had shown no faith at all in the claim at the beginning.

Later, Delaverne professed disbelief when I told him the truth about my initial lack of faith in the Queen. He had a Frenchman's way of accepting an accomplished fact without wondering how it had come about.

The morning Davidson and Fulgham discovered ore in the west drift, Fulgham told me about it when he came out to get a pickeypokey, a tool for drilling extremely soft ground.

I began to question him about the drill in his bunk in what I thought was a calm, fair manner. He gave me an insolent smile and said: "You should talk. You sleep with a pick handle. Your precious little brother has a drill too, and Davidson's got a new candlestick."

With effort I held my anger back. "You're afraid of Davidson, is that it?"

"He started it."

Danny came in with his temper high. He shoved three drills at me, and I saw that the bits had mushed. "What kind of tool dressing do you call that?" he asked.

I grabbed the drills from him so hard that one of the mushroomed heads tore his hand. He cursed angrily. I threw the steel into the dull pile near the slack tub. "There's a good temper on the drill you've got in your bunk," I said.

"Do something about Davidson's candlestick, and we won't have to keep drills in our bunks," Danny answered. He wiped his bleeding hand on his jumper and glared at me.

We wrangled for a full half-hour, the three of us, barely keeping outside the rim of violence. During that time someone came out with the car and went to the dump. Danny and Fulgham said it was my fault Davidson had a candlestick in his bunk. I told them to get out of the shop and go back to work.

They went out. A moment later I heard Danny shout with terrible urgency. I ran from the shop.

Snow was blowing viciously across the dump. Danny and Fulgham were on their hands and knees in the track trench where it turned across the timberyard. When I got to them I saw Charley.

Perhaps he had tried to crawl to the shop. From the way he lay, with his head and shoulders against the side of the trench, with the snow gathered in the wrinkles of his jumper, we knew he had been there some time, perhaps half of the time while we were quarreling in the shop. He must have cried out to us, trying to make us hear above the noise of the wind and the sounds of our own bickering.

We did not want to admit that he was dead. We

carried him into the cabin. I sent Danny to the mine to get Davidson. When they returned, Danny said: "The car is at the end of the track, still loaded. He started to lift it and that was all."

Davidson slumped against the wall. "He must have dropped right there at the car where you found him."

Danny and Fulgham and I did not have the guts to say that if we had not been quarreling in the shop we might have heard Charley's cries for help; we might have saved him. I blamed myself for his death. I never should have brought him up Bulmer Peak. Now I felt the full burden of clashing personalities pressing on me alone.

Tears ran down Fulgham's and Danny's cheeks, and Lenore sat at the table, put her head on her arms, and wept.

We wrapped Charley in blankets and buried him in the deep snow on the dump. The howling wind tried to fill the grave as fast as we shoveled snow from it.

When we stumbled back to the cabin, I realized the full extent of our loss. In the expressions around me, I saw the knowledge that the best of us was gone, and that it was up to us alone to bear our responsibilities as civilized human beings. I knew, too, that each of us doubted his fitness for the task.

When I opened the log that evening, everything I had written in it seemed insignificant. I knew that the Creole Queen was a mere burrow that would be worked out, that its gold would be scattered, and that Bulmer Peak would slowly fill the hole. Work in granite would perish, but the warmth of Charley's life would live. It was like a thin, glowing chain that could not be broken.

I wished to write what I felt in some manner that would stand as a tribute to him. After long pondering I was wise enough to know how ignorant I was. I wrote:

*March 15—Charley Spence died of a heart attack.*

Three days later I remembered to enter in the log the fact that we had struck ore in the west drift.

# Chapter 15

CHARLEY SPENCE was not gone. Some men die and for a time you look on where they once sat or walked or worked, or at odd moments their faces flash in remembrance and you are mildly saddened or even startled to recall that they have vanished. Then the periods of remembering come only occasionally, and at last even the names of the dead slip from memory.

It was not so with Charley. He was too gentle a man to die. His influence planted something in our lives that continued to grow. He left to each of us something individually, not one common memory based on anything he had done to achieve greatness.

We missed him. Sometimes I thought he was sitting at the table. Twice the feeling was so strong that I looked up to see him, to speak to him. I put it down to nerves; but that was not right, for in later years old Charley was close to me many times.

Fulgham and Danny went back together as a drilling team. They left Davidson alone in the west drift. One morning when I went in to see him, Davidson told me in his literal, solemn way: "When I get all wrought up about things, I think Charley is working here beside me, like when we first started. Is that a bad sign, Craig?"

In the smoky candlelight I saw Davidson more clearly than I ever had. I remembered the toy steam engine of long ago; I remembered a boy who was wistful and hurt, but who had never been jealous or mean.

"That's a good sign, Frank. Sometimes I think old Charley is still close by."

"He was a wonderful man, wasn't he?"

"Yes."

"I wish I'd asked him to help me with Lenore."

"How do you mean?"

"Just to talk to her, I guess."

"What about?"

"She's going to leave me, Craig."

Davidson was holding his single jack. He lifted it slowly and tapped the face of it against the palm of his left hand. "Sometimes I wish it had been me instead of Charley."

"How do you know she's going to leave you?" I asked. "Did she say so?"

Davidson shook his head. "I know it, though. I've lost her, Craig. What's the matter with me?"

"Nothing. Maybe you're imagining things."

Again he shook his head slowly, tapping the five-pound hammer into the palm of his big hand. "I know," he said.

"Is that what you're all wrought up about—the times when you think Charley is here, I mean?" It was awkward. I was probing dangerous ground and knew it.

Davidson let the single jack down at his side. He looked at me in the dim light, and I knew that he no longer wanted to talk to me about his troubles. When I went down the drift I knew he was looking at me across his shoulder, standing there quietly, holding the hammer.

I turned at the junction and did not go to see Danny and Fulgham. The Creole Queen was a strong, safe refuge, but now the poisonous influence from the cabin was getting into it.

In the mine I didn't miss Charley nearly as much as in the cabin. I had taken up with his books, fumbling my way through them, trying to learn something of Charley himself, figuring, I suppose, that what he had been was in some measure due to influences that I too could share.

If Danny and Fulgham had been gentlemanly in their courtship of Lenore, their masks were slipping now. They snarled at each other. Sometimes their language fell to a low level before Lenore, and then I reprimanded them savagely in terms that were almost as bad as their own.

Lenore was not on my side, for all I knew was violence. She attempted to do what Charley had done, to shame us, to make us think, to make us act as human beings should behave. She tried, but because she was the reason for the animosity among us her efforts were to no avail.

It was possible that Danny and Fulgham would try to kill each other. I cursed them and prayed for an early spring.

And there was Davidson, completely withdrawn now, not appearing to know what was going on, but seeing everything nevertheless. Every time he went near his bunk I watched him sharply; and when he rolled in, turning with his face close to the candlestick stuck into the wall, I wondered what he was thinking.

There were nights when I rose at odd hours and went outside, sniffing the air for signs of a break in the weather. If no wind was scudding across the snowfields, I could see the twinkle of an occasional light in the valley, a beacon from a friendly, normal world; or the oil headlamp on an ore train coming toward Colorow would show hazily in the night on the long stretch of tangent below Papoose Creek, and I would watch until it was gone, waiting to hear the whistle of the train at Sawmill Junction. Though it was a sad, distant sound, it linked me to my fellow human beings below.

Ever since Charley had asked me if I thought I loved Lenore, I had been trying to answer the question. It was like many of the questions he had asked so gently: they left you uncertain, searching out yourself. I was jealous of Danny's and Fulgham's attentions to Lenore, and I was jealous of the fact that she was married to Davidson. My own hard-headed doubts very nearly convinced me that I was in love with Lenore. I had to make a decision.

One morning, as soon as the others were in the mine, I went to the cabin. Lenore was washing the dishes. I leaned against the edge of the stove, drinking a cup of coffee.

She asked, "How soon can we go down?"

"I don't know. Why?"

"Before the end of the month we're going to be out of food, no matter how I skimp. That's one reason. Do you want others?"

It was April. The grub problem had been worrying me too, and the others certainly could not have been unaware of it. I said: "We'll get a thaw and a hard freeze one of these times. If we don't, there's still the burro."

"Major!" Lenore gave me a horrified look.

"Starving people have done worse."

She accepted that, but she gave me the rough edge of another thought. "You weren't thinking of food when you bullied Frank into dressing out Major."

"No. I acted like an animal, but the fact remains we've got a cache of meat in good condition because I did."

Lenore's dark eyes sparkled with a thoughtful kind of anger. "You find a way to justify everything you do, don't you?"

"It's the only protection I've got against the

193

mistakes I make. Damn it, Lenore, I admitted I was wrong in bullying Frank."

Lenore lifted a battered tin plate from the soapy water and dropped it into the rinsing pan. "You're partly grown up, Craig, and partly still a proud boy."

"You're going to leave Frank?"

"Yes."

"And then?"

"I don't know."

I asked, "Do you love me?"

Lenore gave me a straight look. She shook her head.

It was a jolt. Unsure of my own feelings in the matter, I had cast hers in a way that suited my vanity. She must be lying. But I saw the calmness in her expression and the sureness. No, she was not lying.

"Why did you ask, Craig? Is your sense of duty driving you again?"

"Your husband is the one with the sense of duty, not me. He—"

"Why did you ask me if I loved you?" Lenore said.

"I wanted to know! I have to know so I can tell the proper thing to do if—well, in case—" I had blundered into confirmation of the very thing she had said about my overblown sense of duty. She let me sputter into silence. My pride was hurt. I felt that I had been trapped, and as Lenore watched me with a gentle intentness the feeling increased.

"If I had told you I loved you, Craig, would you have asked me to marry you after I divorced Frank?"

"Yes." I was sullen about it now.

"Why?"

Before Lenore's cool, inquiring expression I could not answer.

"Do you love me, Craig?"

"I don't know. I—" But I could not finish.

She waited, and then said: "But what? You'll marry me because you think you've wronged me. Is that it?"

The advantage had been hers all the way. She knew how to use words and she had known my mind ever since I began to speak. I was old enough to run a mine, tough enough to swagger among men, to fight. I was ambitious and thought well of myself. But Lenore, with her quiet questions, had stripped all that from me and left me feeling young and inept.

"You think you've wronged me, and because of that you're willing to marry me?" Lenore asked.

Anger spoke for me. "Put it your way! Yes, that's it!"

A warmth and an earnestness that I had been too blinded by my vanity to notice earlier left Lenore's face. It was only then that I sensed she had not been tormenting me to prove that she was wiser than I. She had been asking something for herself, not driving me into a corner just for the hell of it.

Suddenly, I wanted to start over again, to answer Lenore's questions free of anger and pride. I tried to force the moment back. "Lenore, perhaps I do love you. It's hard to be sure. You didn't want me to lie when you asked, did you?"

She smiled in a wistful, absent way. It put us ages apart, and told me that I could never go back and start over again.

"No, Craig, you didn't lie. I don't think you'll ever lie about anything."

I had already lied twice to Danny, my own brother. The matter of the stock was nothing; that would come out all right. But I had lied deliberately to him about my relations with Lenore.

"When we go down," I said, "when we're away from this place, you and I—"

"No, Craig."

She didn't tell me to go. She didn't try to explain how I had failed. She simply went on with her work as if I were no longer in the room. I started out. At the door the feeling that Charley was still in the room came to me. As I opened the door I turned to look at the table, knowing of course that I would see only what was actually there, but drawn, nevertheless, and held by the feeling of Charley's undying presence.

As I closed the door I saw that Lenore, standing with her back to me, was crying. I stared a moment and then pushed the door shut and went toward the shop.

The wind was blowing. On the dump where Charley lay beneath the snow the surface was clean and shining. The wind had made little wavelets there, like white sand marked by the rolling of the ocean on a beach.

# Chapter 16

THE MOST DESPERATE time of our whole stay at the Creole Queen came after we saw spring breaking in the valley. Brown fields appeared, and then squares and oblongs of them turned to a richer brown under the plow. We heard the busy whistles of trains plying in and out of Colorow, making up for the time lost when Maria Canyon had been closed with snow.

We were still prisoners. Spring storms blew across us, but their whiteness was wrung out before reaching the valley now coming to green life. Winter was eternal at the Queen.

We ran out of rails for the tunnel. I made shift with lagging poles adzed down to serve as track. Our coal supply, which I had thought more than sufficient, ran low. There were no sacks left outside, and those inside were going fast. The ore pile on the dump had grown tremendously, but the timber pile was almost gone.

On the 26th of April we began to eat the burro.

That should have been an admission that we were indeed in a desperate condition, and perhaps it should have bound us together, but it did not. Everyone hated me because of Major. I hated myself. Davidson would look at the dark meat on his plate and then would stare at me in rebuke for what I had forced him to do.

Danny and Fulgham didn't want to work the mine any longer, but I knew that work was our salvation. I drove them into the Queen every day. Invariably one of them lagged, standing in the doorway of the cabin, talking to Lenore, bending toward her and smiling, saying things the rest of us could not hear.

I would go back and curse the laggard and get him started on his way, but he would stop near the shop, waiting to be sure that *I* did not stay behind at the cabin.

Davidson seemed to be unaware of all this. He plodded off in the lead each day without looking back. But he was not unaware and I knew it. That candlestick at his bunk was like a splinter in my mind.

The 11th of May was our first warm day. You could see the snow yellowing, the fine crystals consolidating into coarse crystals. The snow was settling. Perhaps if the warmth held all day, the penetration of the sun's heat would go deep enough so that freezing that night would make a crust we could walk upon.

No one but Davidson could stay inside. He worked as usual, blinking at us owlishly each time he came from the tunnel into the blinding sunlight with a car of muck. The rest of us, Lenore included, floundered about on the dump, trying to measure the penetration of the sun into the snow, guessing, estimating. There was a holiday spirit among us.

"If it holds hot all day," I said, "by midnight we can walk out of here as if we were walking on dry ground, until we hit the timber, of course."

"Let me get to the timber," Fulgham said, "and no mile or two of snow, no matter how deep, can stop me." For the first time in months he laughed, looking at Lenore as if they shared some secret.

I was planning how to cross the soft snow in the timber. We would take all the blankets and canvas we could carry and two sections of ten-inch boards. We would bridge our way across the soft snow foot by foot, building ahead and tearing up behind. Fulgham's coarse laugh irritated me. When he went over to talk to Lenore, I called him away to help me dig up the boards we needed.

He said: "What's the matter with Danny helping you, Rhodes? He's right beside you."

Danny came plowing through the snow to start a fight. I lashed both him and Fulgham with my temper and sent them into the mine, one at a time.

Lenore turned away from me then and started back to the cabin. I yelled, "What's the matter with you?"

She went on without answering. I was left alone on the dump. We couldn't hold together even when it seemed that deliverance was near. Davidson came out with a load of muck. I watched the deliberate way he pushed it along. Each movement he made was careful and important as he went to the chock. He hooked the safety chain, swiveled the body off its catch, opened the gate and dumped the muck.

He glanced down the dump afterward as if to be sure that every little rock had rolled to a prearranged position.

God damn the stolidness of him anyway!

In the afternoon banks of clouds came up like damp smoke from the west. They drifted across the sun, thinning its power. Water dripped slower and slower from the eaves of the cabin and the shop, and then stopped dripping. The snow began to freeze, but the crust was thin.

We were not leaving the mountain for a while yet.

I walked back and forth along the track, ready to curse like a madman. In the red mists of my senseless anger Charley's face came before me. One time when Danny and I were kids, we were going fishing with him, clear over on the Tomichi. He had hired a rig for the day and we had planned the trip a long time. At four o'clock of the morning we were to leave it was raining so hard we couldn't see out of the east window of the shack. Danny and I whined and howled about the unfairness of it all, the dirty, stinking rain that had come deliberately to ruin our fishing trip. Old Charley listened to us for a time and then said quietly, "Do you boys know some way we can change the weather?" He was never sarcastic. We took his question literally for an instant.

Like so many things Charley had said that did not take hold instantly, his simple question came back to me. I was striding along the track like a fool, berating the elements. I stopped wasting energy and went to work shoveling out the boards we would need when we started our trip down.

At seven o'clock that evening brittle cold settled for the night on Bulmer Peak, but the snow crust was still not strong enough.

We went to bed early, tired from the reaction of soaring hopes that had gone high and then crashed when the clouds drifted across the sun. For the first time since fall I felt a sort of peace. It seems to me now that the afternoon marked the first step I took toward grasping the calm, enduring philosophy of Charley's life.

I slept more soundly than I had for a long time, and yet my conditioning in uneasiness asserted itself when Davidson rose at some time during the night. I heard him get up, but before I opened my eyes he had already crossed the light from the south window and was at the water bucket. He made slow gulping sounds as he drank.

I almost drifted back to sleep. We would be leaving the mine in a few days. Davidson must be as anxious as the rest of us to get down, so there was nothing much to worry about if he got up and prowled the cabin like a slow, nervous animal. With drowsy pleasure I held the fact that Danny and I would go down the hill rich men.

Davidson put the dipper back into the bucket. I heard the faint *glubbing* of water filling it before the dipper sank to the bottom. He did not go back to his bunk. He went down the room past Danny and Fulgham. I could see him only dimly. He went past the bunks across the room, and I thought he was going to the storeroom.

Danny was snoring, softly for once. Fulgham was quiet as Davidson passed him. Ordinarily both Danny and Fulgham would have been wide awake the instant anyone came near their bunks at night. Let Davidson go on into the storeroom, I thought.

He stopped short of the door and turned back, his bare feet padding on the dirt floor. He hesitated at Fulgham's bunk. I raised my head, staring across the dim room. Davidson went on to Danny's bunk and stopped again.

Something about his dark bulk, his motionlessness and his silence, sent sharp tingles up my spine. I grasped the blankets to hurl them back, ready to leap out and shout a warning at Danny if Davidson stayed near his bunk an instant longer.

Davidson moved on. I began to relax, sagging back into my bunk. He had padded around the cabin before in the dead of night. Now he would go back to bed.

He passed across the light from the south window. He was through it and in darkness before

I realized what I had seen. He was carrying the candlestick in his right hand. The bare outline of it was limned in my mind, the pointed end and the vicious hook standing from the shaft.

"Davidson," I said, and then I heard him coming in a rush toward my bunk.

There was no time to get out of it. I grabbed the pick handle and swung it as he came alongside me. It struck him across the thighs but it did not drive him back.

"You!" he said in a hoarse whisper, and I knew the candlestick was driving toward me. I hurled the blankets up. They saved my life. I heard one of them rip as the hook of the candlestick caught in it and Davidson tore it free.

"You!" he said.

I grabbed blindly with both hands toward the needle-sharp steel that was coming in. He was punching with the point as a man would drive a pencil into a ripe melon. It ripped through my palm and then my left hand closed on his wrist. He was a powerful man but so was I, and I was fighting with primeval desperation.

I got both hands on his wrist. He heaved me back and forth in the bunk, grinding his teeth and sucking in his breath noisily as he tried to stab me.

Danny and Fulgham were piling out of their bunks. Lenore called out from the storeroom.

I tried to twist the candlestick out of Davidson's grip. That was when the hook sank deeply into my wrist joint. He heaved back to break my grip. I could not hold him. The hook disjointed my wrist before it tore free. Davidson fell back against the table, and then Danny and Fulgham were coming in on him.

Excitement and the darkness betrayed us all.

I got out of the bunk with my left hand worthless. An elbow smashed me in the mouth, and I struck out angrily with the pick handle. I hit somebody. We became a confused mass of grunting, cursing, struggling men. I shouted, "It's Davidson!"

In the crashing fight along the table nobody knew who was who. I myself struck any man who was close. It may have been my pick handle that cracked two of Danny's ribs. Then the weapon was wrenched from my hand and somebody knocked me part way under a bunk. I grappled with legs that came against me. The man kicked me in the face but I threw him. We wrestled on the cold floor. It was not until my right hand felt crisp, curling whiskers that I knew I was struggling with Fulgham.

I hit him once more after that.

He had me on my back and his thumbs were digging toward my eyes when Lenore held a lamp high and shouted at us.

We got up slowly, the animal heat still surging in our blood. One of the lamps on the table had been smashed, and Danny had coal oil in his eyes. He was leaning on the table, wiping his underwear sleeve across his face.

The door was open and Davidson was gone.

"What happened? Where's Frank?" Lenore held the lamp and stared at us.

"Frank!" I said. "The son of a bitch tried his best to kill me!" I raised my left hand and looked at it. Blood from my ripped palm was mixed with dirt from the floor. The wrist bone was displaced at a weird angle. A quarter-inch of the point of the candlestick hook was broken off clear down in the bone, although I didn't know it at the time.

Fulgham went over and closed the door. When he turned to come back, I saw that the right side of his underwear was soaked with blood. Davidson had embedded the broken hook so deep into the heavy chest muscle that Fulgham's struggle had torn it from his hand.

"He's out there in the snow." Fulgham looked at Lenore.

She put the lamp down. "What are you going to do?"

"Let him freeze!" I said. I tugged on my wrist. The pain was sickening.

Danny turned away from the table and stumbled blindly toward the washstand, still rubbing his eyes.

"He's crazy," I said. "I've gone after him twice before. Now he can freeze."

Fulgham shook his head like a man of wisdom. "We've got to go after him."

I went over to Danny. He had slopped water into the washpan and was soaping his face, cursing under his breath. "You all right, Danny?"

"Hell, yes, outside of being blind! What got into Davidson anyway?" He rinsed the soap away and came up red-eyed and blinking. At once he threw the water on the sacks of coal and poured a fresh pan and began to wash his eyes again.

Lenore went back into the storeroom. She lit a lamp, and I knew she was dressing. Fulgham began to put on his clothes.

I began to dress one-handed. My wrist was a fury of pain. "I'll go with you, Fulgham, but my only reason is to get a good swing at him with a drill."

"In that case, stay here, Rhodes."

Fulgham suddenly was in command. I couldn't say how I had lost my authority, but I knew that his purpose was stronger than mine.

Lenore came to the storeroom. "I'm ready."

Fulgham said, "No, you stay here."

Somehow I knew that she would obey. I struggled into my jacket. Danny had washed his face a third time, but the coal oil was still burning his eyes. He said, "Wait a minute," but we went out and left him.

It was a still, cold night. You could feel the crackling quality of the air. The peaks and the snowfields were blue-white under the starlight. Our breath smoked into the night. We heard the wind door banging at the portal.

"He went in the mine," Fulgham said.

I thought of the long, dark tunnel, the branching drifts, and the dust-soft silence of the Queen. It was the last place I wanted to look for a wild man. Fulgham led off without hesitation.

We went down the snow trench toward the portal. We saw Davidson then. He was sitting in the snow close to where we had put old Charley. He was just sitting there, with his head bent. I gripped the piece of steel hard in my good hand.

We stood there looking at Davidson. I must admit that Fulgham was calm enough about it. He said: "Frank, you'll freeze your hind end off. Come on over here."

Davidson raised both hands and covered his face.

Fulgham waited a moment and then waded out into the snow. The light crust snapped and popped. I followed him a few steps and then circled out to come in on the other side of Davidson. He paid no attention to us as we crunched up close to him.

Suddenly he was crying, weeping like a little child; only, it was a man's voice that made the sounds.

Fulgham reached down and touched him on the shoulder. "Come on, Frank; it's all right. Nobody's hurt."

I dropped the drill into the snow.

"Why'd you come here, Frank?" Fulgham asked.

"Charley," Davidson said. "He was my friend."

"He was a friend to all of us, if we had only known it," Fulgham said. "Let's go inside, huh, Frank?"

Davidson looked up at me. "Craig, I tried to kill you."

"Maybe you should have," I said. "Let's go inside."

Davidson rose from the snow like a weary man who has no place to go. He glanced toward the cabin as if he were about to protest going there. He pushed our hands away when we started to take his arms. We went back to the cabin together, and he was the first one inside. Lenore made a pot of tea for him, and he sat at the table drinking it, paying no attention to the rest of us as we treated our injuries.

Danny pulled on my wrist in an effort to get it back in place. It was swelling so badly we could not tell whether it went back in place or not. Davidson's candlestick had skewered the muscle of Fulgham's chest brutally, making two holes. Danny had cracked ribs and a gashed head where someone had broken the lamp on his skull, and his eyes were red from coal oil.

Davidson drank the tea and then went to bed. After they salved their injuries Danny and Fulgham retired. I spent the rest of the night in a chair. I was no longer afraid of Davidson, but the pain in my wrist was too much for me to consider going to bed. Wedged deep in the joint, the broken end of the candlestick hook was prying up hell, and it was to be much worse later.

I watched Lenore sitting beside Davidson's bunk. Now and then he looked at her with a faint smile and I got the impression that he was close to her for the first time, and that he had made some decision about her that gave him peace.

Her face had taken on fullness in the last few months, and there was something in her expression that troubled me. Men's clothing made her look out of shape. Suddenly I remembered something that I had had no time to think about before. When she lit the lamp while we were fighting, she had been wearing a muslin nightgown and it had twisted tight against her body as she leaned across the table to look down at me and Fulgham.

That was when I had seen the swelling of her belly.

I got up and went down the room to her. I doubted that Danny and Fulgham were asleep, but I didn't care. "Lenore, are you pregnant?"

She gave me a look that seemed to scorn my slow perception. She nodded, and then her expression edged off into remoteness that excluded me, and she looked down at the face of her sleeping husband.

Fulgham said softly, "Of course she is, Rhodes."

I went over to Danny's bunk. He was awake. His eyes were bitter as he looked at me, and then he turned away as he used to do when he was small and did not wish to hear what I was saying.

Sometime during the night I added to the entry I had made earlier in the evening:

*We must get down soon.*

# Chapter 17

THREE days later there was a crust on the snow that would hold us. While we were getting ready to leave we saw a snowslide run in the channel of a peak across the chasm south of us. We heard the breaking of it and saw the slow-gathering force. The slide jumped the confines of the channel and ripped into the timber on the lower slopes of the mountain, smashing trees, leaving a quarter-mile-wide path of ruin.

Davidson stared at it with fascination. "A man wouldn't stand a chance in the middle of that."

"We'll take our chances," I said. My whole left arm was a shaft of pain. My wrist was so swollen that the hand looked small, like the head of a hooded cobra.

Davidson kept staring where the slide had run while the rest of us continued to assemble the gear we would need for the trip down.

We took two sections of slatted-together boards to serve as snow pontoons. We put canvas and blankets in long rolls across our shoulders. We took an ax, a pick, and three shovels.

I led the way. It was an overcast day, ideally suited to our purpose. For a time after we left the toe of the dump, we didn't trust the snow, expecting to break through at every step; but the crust held firm.

We were at the High Place in a short time.

Here we had a chance to estimate the snow depth on the bench, for the High Place was a windy point where little snow had held. The way down to the crossing was a sloping ramp. Estimating the angle and depth of it, I concluded that the snow must be fifteen feet deep on the bench.

The entire crossing was a mass of glittering ice slanting out from the wall and running over the outside edge of the narrow trail. Today you could see into Warner Basin, nine hundred feet below. Because of all the whiteness our ability to perceive depth was inaccurate; the drop did not look nearly as far as it was.

I had the pick. I began to ease myself down the ramp to the trail. Danny took the tool from me and went ahead. "You'd be a lot of use against that ice with one arm," he said. There was no bantering in his voice; there hadn't been for a long time.

Lenore and I sat on a roll of canvas and watched the others taking turns picking the ice. Sometimes it came loose in big chips, glittering with pale blue light as it spilled over the edge. They did not try to chip it down to rock, but only to make a fairly level trail about eighteen inches wide. As they worked ahead they put down a folded blanket. The wool froze quickly to the ice and made good footing.

I sat there thinking of how Charley had steadied

Fulgham on that trail with the touch of his hand and a smile. For some reason I had no fear of the crossing today. I kept holding my injured arm at the elbow. It was sore as a boil on the inside of the elbow, and there was a growing knot of pain in the armpit, and red streaks had begun to extend from the wrist upward.

"I'm worried about your arm, Craig," Lenore said.

"It'll be all right once Dr. Wheeler gets hold of it." I noticed how tired Lenore looked. She was heavily bundled. Her feet were wrapped in gunny sacks. She kept her eyes on her husband even when she was talking to me.

"Whose baby is it?" I asked.

But she would not answer me.

"Are you still going to leave Frank?"

She did not answer that either; but I got the impression that she had changed her mind about leaving him. She kept watching Davidson with a worried expression.

I said, "If you do leave him, I want to marry you."

"Yes, I believe you would, Craig." Lenore's voice was as bleak as the ice below us.

They chopped around a bend in the trail, one man working while the other two waited where the sloping snow met the crossing. Fulgham slipped as he started out on the narrow path of folded blankets. My heart jumped. I heard Lenore gasp.

Fulgham caught his balance and laughed.

When it was Davidson's turn to wait, he stood passively, looking out across Warner Basin. Danny was always restless, beating his hands to warm them, kicking at the snow. When Fulgham was waiting, he kept glancing up at Lenore and me.

The High Place held us up about two hours. Danny chopped out the last of the ice and called from the far side. Lenore and I slid the boards down to where Fulgham and Davidson were standing. Motion made me dizzy for a time, but I was clear-headed enough when I scrambled down to the beginning of the crossing.

Davidson was holding the pontoons upright beside him. He motioned us on. Fulgham looked at me with a trace of his old sneer. "Can you make it, Rhodes?"

I ignored him. "Hold on to my coat," I said to Lenore. "Step where I step."

"I'll take her across," Fulgham said.

He did that, safely and surely, with her holding to his hand. Davidson nodded for me to cross. I was careful, but there was no terror in me this time. Davidson came on with the boards. He went back and began to pull up the blankets and canvas we had walked on. Danny and Fulgham went out and helped him, passing the blankets back to Lenore and me. Some of the material stuck fast and ripped.

The passage was completed. Ahead of us, past Coney Hollow, was the long stretch of mountain where I had seen the frozen breakers of snow last winter. That whole area lay exposed to the south, and we knew the crust would be good.

Davidson walked back on the trail. I thought there must be a blanket left and he was going after it.

Lenore said, "Frank!" He paid no attention. She cried his name again, this time with terror in her voice.

He stopped about thirty feet away. He looked across Warner Basin as if there was something on the mountains that demanded attention.

At the last second I knew what was in his mind.

Davidson rebuked no one with word or gesture. He did not lunge or jump. He merely took one step off the edge of the trail and went to his death as simply as passing from one room to another.

There was no sound.

I knelt at the edge of the trail. He was sprawling in the air, a living human being. His hat blew off. He struck the jutting rock of a ledge that he would have missed if he had leaped from the trail. He bounced from that, suddenly all shapeless and no longer a man, and fell another three or four hundred feet.

A white puff of snow exploded where he struck. The wind across the up-swooped drifts of Warner Basin blew the smoke of the disturbance away, and then all the whiteness blended together again. The whole thing was completed in seconds.

I stared at the others. Danny's face was blank; he was as shocked as I was. And then he turned away from me. Fulgham was steadying Lenore with his arm around her. For just an instant Fulgham and I were fellow human beings sharing the sudden jolt of a companion's death, and then he too accused me with his eyes.

Lenore kept staring at the place where Davidson had been standing moments before.

Her voice broke hysterically as she cried: "We've got to help him! We've got to get down there to him!"

"We can't get down there." I had seen him hit the ledge, and then the snow; even if we could have climbed down into the basin, it would have been a useless mission.

For a while Lenore lost control of her emotions. She clung to Fulgham, and Fulgham helped her to steady herself.

Then we went on.

We did not get down that day; soft snow in the timber was too much. We planked over it foot by foot with the pontoons, until sometime in the afternoon the boards broke and left us almost helpless in twenty-two feet of snow. By using the canvas and the blankets as a mat we managed to cut the tops of trees to make a platform on the snow.

We did not even consider returning to the Queen.

Huddled in wet blankets, we camped that night on the platform. That was when my arm got to me in savage earnest. When dawn came I stupidly tried to walk straight across the snow, stepping boldly off the platform. I plunged down into darkness, fighting the cold suffocation of the fine snow.

Danny and Fulgham had a rough time getting me out.

We made pontoons of limbs and canvas, but that, and the rest of the trip, is vague in my mind. I remember tumbling down a wet snowbank into a road churned to mud by wagon wheels. It was the road to the Eclipse Standard, though I did not recognize it. A mule-skinner with a load of concentrates came down it.

Then we were going toward town on the wagon and the jolting so hurt my arm that I fought with Danny and Fulgham when they kept me from jumping down to walk.

Later I heard Dr. Wheeler say: "Blood poisoning, yes. I'll have to take the arm off, Danny." I began to fight again. They weren't going to get my arm. I put my back against the wall and fought across the bed with my feet.

Then there was a long darkness.

# Chapter 18

LENORE came to see me just once. That was in the middle of the summer and I was still in the hospital, for after the amputation of my arm I almost died from postoperative pneumonia. Only two days earlier a party led by Danny had recovered Davidson's body from Warner Basin, and he was now buried beside Charley in the Colorow cemetery.

Lenore wore no black; she was not the kind to pretend, even for appearance. Calmly she told me that she was going to marry Fulgham that afternoon and that they were leaving on the evening train.

I argued violently against her marrying Fulgham.

Her calm determination never wavered, although there were several long moments when she watched me quietly, as if waiting and listening for something greater than my angry objections.

That was the last time I ever saw her. When I heard the whistle of the train that evening it was a lonely, haunting sound that still comes back to me in the quiet hours of the night.

Before fall stock in the Creole Queen went from ten cents a share to fourteen dollars a share. Danny took his money and went to Mexico, where he lost everything in a silver mine. I never saw him again after he left Colorow. He was a sergeant in the Army when he died in Manila in 1898.

Bonnie Bannerman and I were married when I got out of the hospital.

I still have the log of the Creole Queen, which for a short time was the wonder of the mining world. Delaverne glanced briefly at a few entries in the log when I offered it to him. He frowned and riffled the pages like a deck of cards. "This tells only how you found the gold?"

"That's all."

"Nothing of the things which happened day by day among five men and one woman all alone—"

"No! Just the story of the mine."

His shrug was a gesture which said that I was incomprehensible. "No wonder she went away," he murmured, and afterward denied that there was any meaning in his remark.

Delaverne married his childhood sweetheart in France and they settled in San Francisco. I assumed that his wife would be an exotic woman, but she was a dumpy, practical housewife who bore him five sons and made him very happy. To hear him tell it, one of the greatest disappointments of his life was my refusal to relate the personal details of what happened during that wild winter at the Queen.

All of them who were with me at the Queen are gone now. Only dimming memory can recall them, memory that grows clearer when I open the log. To an outsider it tells little, but to me it brings back the wind, the snowfields hanging fiercely white on the great mountain, the crackling tension in the big room of the cabin, the faces of Lenore and Danny, never older than when I last saw them, and sad remembrance of my own youthful arrogance.

The years that have made the pages fragile have also absorbed all my hatred of Fulgham. Far more important, time has made Charley Spence stronger and clearer. Not just the man alone, but everything that he stood for, emerges firm and undying from the faded writing in the log of the Creole Queen.

**Steve Frazee** was born in Salida, Colorado, and for the decade 1926–1936 he worked in heavy construction and mining in his native state. He also managed to pay his way through Western State College in Gunnison, Colorado, from which in 1937 he graduated with a Bachelor's degree in journalism. The same year he also married. He began making major contributions to the Western pulp magazines with stories set in the American West as well as a number of North-Western tales published in *Adventure*. Few can match his Western novels which are notable for their evocative, lyrical descriptions of the open range and the awesome power of natural forces and their effects on human efforts. *Cry Coyote* (1955) is memorable for its strong female protagonists who actually influence most of the major events and bring about the resolution of the central conflict in this story of wheat growers and expansionist cattlemen. *High Cage* (1957) concerns five miners and a woman snowbound at an isolated gold mine on top of Bulmer Peak in which the twin themes of the lust for gold and the struggle against the savagery of both the elements and human nature interplay with increasing, almost tormented intensity. *Bragg's Fancy Woman* (1966) concerns a free-spirited woman who is able to tame a family of thieves. *Rendezvous* (1958) ranks as one of the finest mountain man books and *The Way Through the Mountains* (1972) is a major historical novel. Not surprisingly, many of Frazee's novels have become major motion pictures. According to Bill Pronzini in the second edition of *Twentieth Century Western Writers,* a Frazee story is possessed of 'flawless characterization, particularly when it involves the clash of human passions; believable dialogue; and the ability to create and sustain damp-palmed suspense.' His latest novel to appear is *Hidden Gold,* published as a Five Star Western.

**Center Point Publishing**
600 Brooks Road ● PO Box 1
Thorndike ME 04986-0001 USA

**(207) 568-3717**

**US & Canada:**
**1 800 929-9108**
www.centerpointlargeprint.com